It was becoming more and more obvious by the moment that he could never have a superficial romance with Kirsten Reinhold.

He wasn't sure what it was about her that attracted him so, but he meant to put a stop to it before things got out of control.

He should have let well enough alone right from the beginning and stayed away from her. But no, he had to play with fire and pursue her.

He'd known that the feelings she aroused in him were dangerous, but instead of facing that fact and beating a hasty retreat he'd denied it. He'd told himself she was a sexy lady and he was single and available. If they lit sparks off one another, fine. If not, there was no harm done.

No harm? Ha! He'd vastly overestimated his ability to casually light a fuse without setting off a bomb.

D0354005

Dear Reader,

This April, let Silhouette Romance shower you with treats. We've got must-read miniseries, bestselling authors and tons of happy endings!

The nonstop excitement begins with Marie Ferrarella's contribution to BUNDLES OF JOY. A single dad finds himself falling for his live-in nanny—who's got a baby of her own. So when a cry interrupts a midnight kiss, the question sure to be asked is *Your Baby or Mine?*

TWINS ON THE DOORSTEP, a miniseries about babies who bring love to the most unsuspecting couples, begins with *The Sheriff's Son*. Beloved author Stella Bagwell weaves a magical tale of secrets and second chances.

Also set to march down the aisle this month is the second member of THE SINGLE DADDY CLUB. Donna Clayton, winner of the prestigious Holt Medallion, brings you the story of a desperate daddy and the pampered debutante who becomes a *Nanny in the Nick of Time*.

SURPRISE BRIDES, a series about unexpected weddings, continues with Laura Anthony's *Look-Alike Bride*. This classic amnesia plot line has a new twist: Everyone believes a plain Jane is really a Hollywood starlet— including the actress's ex-fiancé!

Rounding out the month is the heartwarming *A Wife for Doctor Sam* by Phyllis Halldorson, the story of a small town doctor who's vowed never to fall in love again. And Sally Carleen's *Porcupine Ranch,* about a housekeeper who knows nothing about keeping house, but knows exactly how to keep her sexy boss happy!

Enjoy!

Melissa Senate
Senior Editor
Silhouette Romance

Please address questions and book requests to:
Silhouette Reader Service
U.S.: 3010 Walden Ave., P.O. Box 1325, Buffalo, NY 14269
Canadian: P.O. Box 609, Fort Erie, Ont. L2A 5X3

A WIFE FOR DR. SAM

Phyllis Halldorson

Silhouette

R O M A N C E™

Published by Silhouette Books

America's Publisher of Contemporary Romance

If you purchased this book without a cover you should be aware
that this book is stolen property. It was reported as "unsold and
destroyed" to the publisher, and neither the author nor the
publisher has received any payment for this "stripped book."

For all you talented writers and teachers who have
been in critique groups with me over the years, and
have given so unstintingly of your time and expertise
to set me on the right track and keep me there. I won't
attempt to name you, but I know who you are and I am
grateful beyond words.

 SILHOUETTE BOOKS

ISBN 0-373-19219-3

A WIFE FOR DR. SAM

Copyright © 1997 by Phyllis Halldorson

All rights reserved. Except for use in any review, the reproduction
or utilization of this work in whole or in part in any form by any
electronic, mechanical or other means, now known or hereafter
invented, including xerography, photocopying and recording, or in
any information storage or retrieval system, is forbidden without
the written permission of the editorial office, Silhouette Books,
300 East 42nd Street, New York, NY 10017 U.S.A.

All characters in this book have no existence outside the imagination of
the author and have no relation whatsoever to anyone bearing the same
name or names. They are not even distantly inspired by any individual
known or unknown to the author, and all incidents are pure invention.

This edition published by arrangement with Harlequin Books S.A.

® and TM are trademarks of Harlequin Books S.A., used under license.
Trademarks indicated with ® are registered in the United States Patent
and Trademark Office, the Canadian Trade Marks Office and in other
countries.

Printed in U.S.A.

PHYLLIS HALLDORSON

met her real-life Prince Charming at the age of sixteen. She married him a year later, and they settled down to raise a family. A compulsive reader, Phyllis dreamed of someday finding the time to write stories of her own. That time came when her two youngest children reached adolescence. When she was introduced to romance novels, she knew she had found her long-delayed vocation. After all, how could she write anything else after living all those years with her very own Silhouette hero?

○   ○   ○

COPPER CANYON, IDAHO, HOSPITAL RECORDS

Patient's Name: Kirsten Reinhold

Age: 26

Occupation: nurse

++This section for physician's comments only.++

Outward Symptoms:

Patient appears quite lovely,
actually. Her sweet smile and
vivacious personality are utterly
contagious. She positively glows.

History:

First met patient through a
matchmaking scheme that backfired.
Now *my* heart rate is climbing—and
I'm having trouble breathing.

Prognosis:

Marry this woman...STAT!

Signed: ___~Dr. Sim~___   **Date:** _____

Chapter One

The road sign on the outskirts of Grangeville, Idaho, read: Copper Canyon, 10 Miles, and Kirsten Reinhold's excitement mounted. According to the directions Coralie had sent, the Buckley family farm was five miles on the other side of the small town of Copper Canyon so that meant she would arrive at her destination in about twenty minutes.

She pressed her foot harder on the gas pedal. This was the day she'd looked forward to for more than two months. She would see her best friend, Coralie Dixon, and finally meet Coralie's new husband, Jim Buckley.

A loud roar of static interrupted the country-music program on the car radio and startled Kirsten. There were no other cars on the road, and she slowed down to look at the dashboard for the off knob when a sudden impact jolted her forward and sent her car skidding across to the opposite side of the road. She was too surprised and shaken to do anything but clench the steering wheel and hope the car would stop before going into the ditch.

It did, just barely, but her mind had gone blank and her fingers seemed to be frozen around the steering wheel.

Badly shaken, she rested her forehead against the rim and tried to pull herself together. That was why she didn't see the man jump out of the automobile she'd hit to rush across the empty road and open her door.

"Are you hurt, miss?" he asked anxiously.

Slowly she straightened up and looked at him. He was fairly young, mid-thirties, with short, curly brown hair and troubled brown eyes flecked with green. "N-no, I don't think so. What...what happened?"

The concern in his expression turned to a frown of annoyance. "You ran a four-way stop and smashed into my brand-new car," he grumbled. "Why don't you watch where you're going?"

She blinked in confusion and looked beyond him to see a white BMW crosswise in the middle of the highway, with a dent in the fender on the passenger side. "But there were no other cars around, and I just glanced down to turn off the radio."

"Then you didn't look closely enough," he scolded. "I was driving on the side road. I saw you coming, but I expected you to stop at the sign." His anger was heating up.

"I didn't see the sign," she wailed. "I had no idea—"

"If you don't start paying more attention to your driving instead of fiddling with the damn radio, you're going to have a real smashup one of these days." His tone was gruff. "Are you sure you're all right?"

"I'm fine," she said, although she knew that wasn't altogether true. She wasn't injured, but she was shaking so badly that she doubted if she could stand.

Then a frightening thought occurred to her. She carried only the minimum amount of car insurance required by law in California where she lived. She doubted it would fully cover any large bills. "How about you? Were you hurt?" she asked, growing concerned.

"No," he snapped. "But if you'd been going just a little

faster we both could have been. Step out of the car, please.''

"Out of the car? But why?'' She didn't really want to try to stand up yet. She was afraid her quaking knees wouldn't hold her.

"Because I need to make sure you have enough wits about you to drive without plowing into any more vehicles,'' he said angrily.

Kirsten knew she was at fault, but he didn't need to be so cranky. "Of course I'm okay to drive,'' she insisted. "We didn't collide very hard.''

To prove her point she turned in her seat and put her feet on the ground, then pulled herself up by hanging on to the open door. Her legs were rubbery and she felt a little light-headed, but she wasn't about to admit it. The quicker she could get rid of this man and be on her way, the better. So far she hadn't seen any other cars go by.

He looked at his watch, muttered something impatiently, then stepped back several feet along the road and called to her. "Walk over here to me.''

This man was getting to be a real pain, she thought. "I told you, I'm just fine. You don't need to worry about me,'' she called huffily.

"Maybe so,'' he answered, "but please do as I say. I have important appointments to keep.''

There was a no-nonsense quality to his tone that indicated he was used to having his orders obeyed, and she was sure it would just be a waste of time to argue.

Taking a deep breath she put one foot in front of the other, then let loose of the door and started toward him. The road surface was rough and her dizziness increased, but she continued to concentrate on not stumbling.

She was almost there when she stepped into a pothole and was thrown off balance. Gasping, she threw out her arms as the man caught her and held her close against him.

Her flailing arms circled his neck and she buried her face in his shoulder and clung.

He was strong and muscular, and there was a faint woodsy aroma about him. She wasn't sure if it was shaving lotion or just the natural scent of the mountain forest.

She was still trembling, but didn't know if it was shock from the collision or pleasure aroused by the protectiveness of his embrace.

But it wasn't an embrace. He was simply holding her up to keep her from falling flat on her face. What on earth was the matter with her anyway? It wasn't as though she'd never been held by a man before.

He didn't seem in any hurry to let her go, but that was probably because he wasn't sure what to do with her.

Reluctantly, she raised her head, unwound her arms and pushed gently away from him. Her dizziness had receded, but still the man kept one arm around her waist as they walked back to her car.

"I...I just stumbled," she assured him. "I really am okay, but thanks for your concern. By the way, shouldn't we exchange names and addresses? My insurance will pay for the damages to your BMW."

As soon as she uttered the words she knew she'd spoken unwisely. She shouldn't have admitted to being at fault until she talked to her insurer.

They reached her four-year-old navy blue Mustang, and he withdrew his arm from around her and reached in his inside coat pocket. "I'm in a hurry," he said as he withdrew a business card and handed it to her. "If you'll just write down your name, address and the name of your insurance company I'll get back to you later. You do live around here, don't you?"

She unzipped her purse and tossed his card inside, then rummaged around until she found a note tablet and pencil. "No, I don't," she answered, "but I'm visiting here for the next few weeks. I'll give you that address, too."

She scribbled the information on a sheet of the tablet, tore it off and folded it, then handed it to him. He shoved it in his pocket then helped her into the car and shut the door. "Start the engine," he said.

She turned the key and the motor purred.

"Looks like it will run okay," he observed. "You go on ahead. I'll stay behind you until we get to Copper Canyon to make sure it doesn't stall." He backed away from the vehicle. "I'll be in touch, and for God's sake watch where you're going."

True to his word he followed behind her until they came to the pretty little village, almost hidden from the road by huge old evergreen and shade trees. Then he turned off on one of the side streets while she kept going on the main artery through the town and beyond.

A few miles later she saw the rural mailbox labeled Buckley and turned onto the long driveway that led to the white two-story farmhouse surrounded by trees. There were several outbuildings, including a big red barn. Everything looked just as Coralie had described it in her letters and phone calls.

Kirsten parked beside the house and got out, but as she came around the back of the car she heard a screen door open and close and Coralie came bouncing down the front steps, a welcome smile on her face and her arms outstretched. The two friends hugged, then leaned back to look at each other.

Kirsten had never seen Coralie look so happy. She positively glowed, and there was no need to ask if her marriage was all she'd expected it to be. It obviously was. Her straight blond hair was still shoulder length and parted in the middle, but now she had it tied back with a scarf, and her deep blue eyes sparkled with happiness.

"You're positively radiant," Kirsten told her. "I guess your pen-pal farmer turned out to be Prince Charming in disguise."

Coralie laughed with delight. "You better believe it," she agreed. "Just wait till you meet him. I've got the perfect man for you, too."

"Oh, no," Kirsten said with a grin. "If you're talking about your husband's best friend, Dr. Sam, whom you've written so much about, you can forget it. I'm not looking to be fixed up with a groom, either homegrown or mail-order. I'm content to bask in your happiness."

"That's nonsense," Coralie said, "and you know it. Happiness isn't contagious, it can't be caught. You have to experience your own, and as I've told you, Sam Lawford is an ideal candidate for a husband. He's almost as handsome as my Jim, plus since he's one of only two physicians in town his financial future is assured. Even more important, he's one of the nicest, most considerate men I've ever met. Next to Jim, of course."

Kirsten opened her mouth to protest, but Coralie's chatter didn't skip a beat. "Besides, everything's all set up. I've invited him for supper tonight so you two can meet. You've only got a month to get to know each other," she added. "There's no time to waste."

Kirsten could see that she might as well accept the inevitable. After all, Coralie was her hostess, so she couldn't very well be rude and refuse to go along with her plans.

"All right," she said, striving for a light tone. "But I work with physicians all the time. Couldn't you have fixed me up with someone different? Maybe a plumber or a banker?"

They both laughed, but Kirsten quickly sobered. "I appreciate what you're trying to do, but please, don't push this matchmaking bit. If there's a special man out there for me I'll find him without anyone's help."

Coralie apparently caught the wariness in Kirsten's voice, and her radiance faded a bit as her gaze roamed more inquiringly over her friend. "You've lost weight," she observed with a frown. "And you didn't have any to lose.

You look pale, Kirsten, and tired. I can see why your doctor wouldn't let you go back to work for another month. Do you still have that last spot of pneumonia on your lung?"

Kirsten grimaced. She didn't like being reminded that she'd been seriously ill during the past two months. "You never forget that you're a nurse, do you?" she grumbled affectionately. "Well, I'm a nurse, too, so please accept the fact I know what I'm talking about when I tell you the virus has been wiped out, the pneumonia is all cleared up and the asthma attacks are under control. The only reason I can't return to work at the hospital right now is because my immune system has been weakened and the doctor doesn't want me exposed to all the germs that float around a medical facility."

"Yeah, well..." Coralie sounded unconvinced. "I'm going to see to it that you get plenty of rest and healthy meals during the month you'll be here. Right now, though, come meet my two beautiful stepdaughters."

Inside the house was just as old-fashioned and homey as it was on the outside. The rooms were large, the ceilings high and the furniture mostly antiques that had been in the family for generations. The air was redolent with the aroma of roasting beef, and Kirsten remembered that they served dinner at midday on the farm.

Coralie proudly introduced her stepdaughters. Gloria was fifteen, tall with dark brown hair and brown eyes, and Amber, at thirteen, was short with blond hair and blue eyes. It wasn't easy to tell who were the daughters and who was the stepmother. It was on the tip of Kirsten's tongue to tease them about it, but she stopped herself just in time when she remembered that the almost thirteen-year age difference between Coralie and her husband was a sore subject with Jim.

According to Coralie he'd fought against falling in love with her because of it, and even though they were now married he was still embarrassed when someone mistook his new wife for one of his daughters.

Instead, she told the girls how pleased she was to meet them, and how much she was looking forward to her visit.

"I know you're eager to meet Jim," Coralie told Kirsten, "but he's out working in the fields. He'll be home in about an hour for dinner, and I've got the pot roast, potatoes and carrots cooking in a roaster in the oven. Gloria and Amber will do the last-minute things, so why don't we go over to Jim's dad's house and get you settled in?"

"I'd love to," Kirsten said enthusiastically. "Are you sure your father-in-law doesn't mind me staying there?"

Coralie's eyebrows rose. "Buck? Of course not. He's happy to have somebody occupying it while he's gone. The only thing he's upset about is that he probably won't be back from his old army buddies' reunion in Missouri in time to meet you."

Coralie had a last-minute discussion about dinner preparations with the girls, then joined Kirsten as they left the house and walked out to the car. It was only then that Coralie noticed the dents in the front fender and grille, which had been partially hidden by the shrubbery along the driveway.

"Kirsten, what happened to your car?" she asked. "Those dents look new."

"They are," Kirsten admitted. "I had a fender bender with another car between here and Grangeville." She went ahead to explain what had happened. "I can't deny it was my fault," she concluded, "and the man I hit was really mad. I just hope my insurance will cover all the damage."

Coralie looked at her askance. "You did exchange names, phone numbers and insurance companies, didn't you? Who was he? Maybe Jim knows him."

"Oh, yeah, we did all that," Kirsten assured her. "He gave me a business card, but I tossed it in my purse without reading it. I'll show it to you later."

The two women took Kirsten's car and drove approximately a city block through wheat fields to a beige cottage neatly trimmed in brown, which was set in the middle of a grove of huge, old shade trees. It was far enough away from the big house for privacy, but close enough to ensure against loneliness.

The cottage was considerably newer than the house and consisted of a living room, kitchen, two bedrooms and a bath. All the rooms were small, but it was ideal for one or two people. Kirsten and Coralie chatted happily as they unpacked Kirsten's suitcases and put her clothes away.

"So, how are things back in Eureka?" Coralie asked as she put a stack of pastel-colored silk panties in a drawer.

"Well, we haven't had any more of those California earthquakes that drove you away," Kirsten answered.

Coralie shivered. "Thank God for that. After losing everything for the third time in six years in that last one, I just couldn't stay in California any longer."

"So you answered an advertisement in a magazine for a mail-order wife and wound up marrying the handsome hunk who placed the ad and living on a farm in Idaho," Kirsten teased.

Coralie laughed. "It wasn't as simple as that, as you very well know, but if I hadn't run away from earthquakes I would never have met the man who turned out to be the love of my life." She sobered. "And Jim is that, Kirsten. I firmly believe we were destined to be together."

Now it was Kirsten who shivered. Was it possible that some couples were bound together by destiny?

Dr. Sam Lawford turned off the shower and reached for a towel, which he rubbed briskly over his trim, wet body, then knotted around his waist. As usual he was running late. He'd hoped to have time to unwind with a leisurely bath and a long, cool drink to revitalize his flagging energy. Instead, Thad Tucker's youngest boy had stumbled while running with a wicked-looking knife in his hand, which his parents didn't know he had, and Sam had spent the hour he'd saved for relaxation cleaning out the cut in the kid's arm and putting five stitches in it.

Now he had just ten minutes to dress and drive out to the Buckley farm, if he was to arrive at the appointed time of six o'clock. Obviously that was impossible. He slapped shaving lotion on his newly shaved face, and rummaged in the dresser drawer for clean underwear.

What he really wanted to do was stay home, fix himself a thick turkey sandwich and stretch out with the new detective novel he'd received from the book club the week before. The last thing he wanted was to go to Jim and Coralie's for supper. He loved Jim like a brother, and Coralie was a real sweetheart when she wasn't singing the praises of her best friend, Kirsten something-or-other, whom he was supposed to meet for the first time tonight.

Sam hated blind dates, and it annoyed him no end when the wives of his friends insisted on playing matchmaker. He was perfectly capable of finding his own companions, and he had no intention of getting married.

He selected a pair of brown slacks and a short-sleeved green plaid shirt to wear. While summers in the mountains of Idaho were fairly mild, it was still too warm to be comfortable in a tie and sport coat. He wasn't out to impress Ms. Whatever-her-name-was.

When he'd finished dressing, he ventured outside and was again jolted by the sight of the crumpled fender on his BMW. He'd only had it for a week, and in that time he'd protected and sheltered it like a baby. Then, in the blink of an eyelid, that sexy young airhead who didn't have sense enough to keep her eyes on the road had run a stop sign and crumpled one side of its shiny white magnificence.

His rage ignited again. She had no business driving a car. She was a menace on the road. Who had issued her a driver's license in the first place?

It was probably a man. All she would have to do was pout and bat her long, thick eyelashes at a man, and he would give her anything she wanted. Sam figured he should know. She'd even had him going there for a while.

When she'd first looked up at him with those wide doe-like eyes, he'd felt a rush of tenderness that took his breath away. She'd looked so shocked and vulnerable, and for a moment he'd had an urge to take her in his arms and assure her that she was innocent of any wrongdoing. That he would take care of everything, if she would just smile at him.

He snorted with self-disgust as he backed the battered car out of the driveway. He'd been so swamped with patients all day that he hadn't even had time to take it to the garage. Fortunately, the damage was only to the body. The V-12 engine still purred like a kitten.

As he drove down the tree-lined streets on his way out of town, his unruly mind returned to the accident and the woman responsible. Her driving skills left a lot to be desired, but her looks sure didn't. Even though he'd been mad as hell at her at the time, he couldn't help but notice her.

She was a real beauty. Quite tall, approximately five-seven to his five-eleven, and she'd fit into his embrace as if she'd been custom-made for him.

A wave of warmth washed over him and he groaned and shifted his thoughts back to the present. Obviously it had been too long since he'd had a date! He'd been so busy that he barely had time for sleep, let alone a social life.

But why was he attracted to this woman he didn't even know?

Because he'd made the mistake of catching her when she stumbled, that was why. She'd snuggled into his arms, so soft, so warm and inviting, and she'd smelled faintly of lilacs, his favorite floral scent. He'd held her close and had a hard time letting her go when she pulled away from him.

Then another thought caught him off balance. Could that fall have been deliberate? Had she been using her femininity to distract him and make him feel protective?

Sure she could have. Not only could have, but probably did. She'd no doubt been bewitching males all her life, to get what she wanted.

Well, he'd learned his lesson early on, and he wasn't going to be caught in that particular hell again. He had good reason to distrust women.

A few minutes later he turned off the two-lane country road onto the Buckleys' driveway. There was the usual assortment of automobiles, trucks and farm machinery scattered around the barnyard, and he paid little attention as he stopped near the front of the house.

Before he got to the top of the steps the screen door was flung open and Coralie walked out grinning happily. "Well, if it isn't the *late* Dr. Sam," she said gaily. "What was it this time? Mandy Hoover's overdue baby, or old Mr. Proctor's rheumatism?"

"Neither one, smarty," he said as he gave her a friendly hug. "It was the Tuckers' youngest son. He fell while running with a knife, and I had to put sutures in his arm. How long before we eat? I'm starved."

Coralie laughed and disengaged herself as she turned toward the door. "I'm not going to feed you until I've introduced you to my best friend in all the world," she said as she walked into the house with Sam right behind her.

The sun was still bright, and it took him a few seconds to adjust his eyes to the darker living room. As he blinked, Coralie indicated a woman who had just risen from the couch and was standing a couple of feet away.

"Sam, I want you to meet my friend, Kirsten Reinhold," she said, and there was excitement in her tone. "Kirsten, this is Sam Lawford, the doctor I've told you so much about."

One final blink cleared Sam's vision, and he saw himself gazing into those same doelike brown eyes that had been haunting him since this morning.

Kirsten Reinhold was the airhead who had trashed his brand-new car!

Chapter Two

"No!"

"No!"

Their denials were spoken in unison, even in perfect harmony, as though a conductor had lowered his baton to signal the first fortissimo notes of a fiery duet.

But this was no duet. It was an anguished protest to a fate that seemed intent on bedeviling two nice, unsuspecting people caught in a web of circumstances through no fault of their own.

"*You* are Kirsten Reinhold? The angel of mercy and paragon of virtue whose praise Coralie has been singing to me for months?" Sam sputtered.

"And *you*... You are Sam Lawford? The world's most eligible bachelor, who only needs the right woman to turn him into the world's most perfect husband?" Kirsten stammered sarcastically. "Why didn't you tell me who you were this morning?"

"Why didn't *I?* I did. I gave you my business card. Why didn't *you* tell me who you were?"

She couldn't believe he could be so obtuse. "I did. I

wrote it all out on a piece of paper and handed it to you. It's not my fault you didn't look at it.''

Her sense of fair play finally caught up with her, and she sighed. ''Although, I...I have to admit I didn't read your card, either.''

A second male voice boomed through the room. ''What's going on here?''

It was Jim Buckley. In the few hours she'd been at the farm, Kirsten found him to be every bit as handsome and loving toward his family as Coralie had said. And he was just plain nice. Now he was standing next to Coralie, and they both looked surprised and perplexed.

Kirsten was the first to offer an explanation. ''This...this is the man who was involved in the accident with me on the road this morning.'' Her tone still rang with resentment.

''She caved in the whole side of my car,'' Sam interjected, angrily.

''I did no such thing.'' Her denial was heated. ''It was only a slight dent in the front fender. The way you carry on you'd think I'd run over one of your children.''

''I don't have any children, but I've only had that car for a week. Six days to be exact,'' he said, fuming. ''I had to go all the way to Boise to find a BMW dealership, and it hardly had a fingerprint on it until you came roaring down the road and rammed into it.''

Kirsten's mouth dropped open. ''Roaring down the road!'' she raged. ''I was barely moving. Twenty miles an hour at the most when you came out of nowhere and drove right in front of me—''

''Whoa there, take it easy!'' Jim interrupted as he stepped between the two combatants. ''Let's cool down a little and find out what really happened.'' He nodded to Kirsten. ''Okay, you first.''

Belatedly Kirsten realized that both she and Sam were being rude, to say nothing of tacky, by waging their quarrel in the home of their host and hostess. She was regretful and embarrassed, but they'd gone too far now not to try to settle it.

She recounted how she'd taken her eyes off the road for just a second to turn off the radio. "I don't know where he came from. There wasn't a car in sight when I looked," she concluded.

"You claim you didn't see the stop sign, either," Sam pointed out, "so you couldn't have even looked to the sides of the road."

Kirsten knew what he said was undoubtedly true, and she would have admitted it if he'd been reasonable. But he wasn't reasonable, so she wasn't going to be either. She'd already apologized, and she wasn't about to do it again.

"I did, too—" she started to insist, but again Jim interrupted.

"Now hold on a minute, both of you." Jim's tone was stern. "Kirsten, you've told your side of the story, now let Sam tell his." He looked at the other man. "Okay, pal, go ahead."

Sam wished he'd used more restraint when he first realized that Coralie's friend and houseguest was the woman who'd bashed in his car. Unfortunately he'd shot off his mouth, and now all he could do was take a deep breath and try to control his aggravation. "I had a full schedule of patients at my office this morning when I had to drop everything and hurry out to Chester Atkinson's farm to help one of his cows deliver a calf that was turned wrong and couldn't be expelled...."

"A calf?" Kirsten broke in, too astonished to be polite. "I thought you were an M.D.!"

He looked at her and nodded brusquely. "I am, but there's only one veterinarian in this whole area, and he had to fly back East a couple of days ago to attend the funeral of a family member, so I was the next best thing. Delivering baby animals isn't that much different from delivering baby humans, and without medical intervention both the cow and the calf would have died.''

Kirsten was stunned by an unexpected rush of admiration for this pugnacious man. She'd worked with a lot of physicians, but she doubted that any of them would have interrupted office hours to make a house call way out in the country to deliver a calf!

''Are they all right?'' she asked softly.

He nodded and smiled. ''Yeah. All the little guy needed was to be repositioned and he popped right out.''

He looked altogether different when he smiled. His cold brown eyes warmed and softened, and his whole expression lightened. For the first time she saw the slight indentations of dimples on either side of his mouth.

Was it possible she'd misjudged him? If he'd had an office full of sick patients waiting for him to return from an emergency house call, it was no wonder he'd been so harried and impatient with her. She'd delayed his return even longer, as well as damaging his new car.

''That...that's very commendable of you, Doctor,'' she said, suddenly shy as she basked in the warmth of his smile. ''I'm a nurse, and I don't know any physicians who make house calls for humans, let alone animals.''

He chuckled, and there was a sensual sound to it that made her tingle. ''I assure you, going to the cow was the only way to handle the situation. Can you just imagine the reaction of my waiting room full of patients if Farmer Atkinson had led his bellowing pregnant bovine into their midst?'' He extended his hand. ''And please, call me Sam.''

She put her hand in his. His was smooth and well cared for, as most doctors' hands were, but it was also hard and muscular and his grip was strong.

Their gazes met, and for the first time he was looking at her as an attractive woman instead of an incompetent ditz who couldn't even steer a car down a deserted highway without running into his new and expensive toy.

"All right, Sam," she said. "And I'm Kirsten. Coralie's told me so much about you that I feel as if I already know you."

He still held her hand, and she couldn't seem to summon the willpower to pull it out of his grasp.

"Did she tell you that I sometimes act like a real jerk?" he asked seriously.

"No, that came as a surprise," she blurted and felt the hot blush of embarrassment stain her face as soon as she realized what she'd said. "Oh, I mean... That is..."

He squeezed her hand and released it. "Don't apologize," he admonished her. "I had that coming. I've been acting like a spoiled five-year-old throwing a tantrum because one of my playthings got broken. I am sorry. I'm not usually so impatient and childish. It must have been the pressure of time constraints. I've been literally running from one patient to another all day long, and I'm afraid I got my priorities screwed up. Will you please forgive me?"

There was a twinkle in his deep-set eyes, and she would have forgiven him anything. "Of course," she agreed readily, "if you'll forgive me for damaging your beautiful car."

He shrugged. "It's nothing a little bodywork won't fix."

He was being amazingly casual about the accident, considering how upset he'd been just a few minutes earlier.

Coralie finally spoke from her position beside Kirsten. "If you two have settled the matter of who did what to whom, we'd better sit down to supper before everything gets cold."

For the next couple of hours Kirsten thoroughly enjoyed herself. The food she and Coralie had prepared was delicious; Jim was a gracious host; his daughters were bright and well mannered, and Dr. Sam Lawford had made a lightning change from ogre to charmer.

Her innate good sense told her she shouldn't be captivated by his illusive charm, but she couldn't help herself. He was seated next to her at the table, and she was again aware of the fresh, clean aroma of the forest that she'd noticed that morning. The scent was uniquely his and it drew her attention no matter how hard she tried to ignore it.

Contrary to Coralie's efforts at matchmaking, Kirsten hadn't come to Idaho to find a groom. Oh, her long-term goal was to settle down with a husband and children, but she'd only recently celebrated her twenty-sixth birthday, and there were still a lot of things she wanted to do before she got to that point.

She wanted to advance in her profession. She loved nursing, and hoped someday to go back to school to become a nurse-practitioner. She also wanted to travel, to see the world a little at a time: Europe, Asia, and especially Scandinavia where her dad's family had its roots. Her parents were middle-class people who had trouble making ends meet, so she'd had to put herself through college with scholarships and part-time jobs.

Now she wanted to be free, but that didn't mean she couldn't date and have fun. Far from it. She had a very satisfactory social life in Eureka and dated often, but never exclusively with one man. She had many male friends, but drew the line at taking any of them as lovers.

Sam finished his strawberry shortcake smothered in fresh whipped cream and sank back with a contented sigh. Coralie had moved the adults into the comfort of the living room before serving dessert, but Gloria and Amber had taken theirs and gone upstairs to watch television in their rooms.

He and Kirsten were seated together on the sofa. If she hadn't been wearing a full-skirted cotton dress that billowed on either side, their hips would have been touching. His thigh muscles twitched at the thought, and it was all he could do to keep his hand from inching over to caress her leg.

He hated to admit it to himself, but his usual keen assessment of people had been really flawed this time. Kirsten Reinhold was neither airheaded nor conniving. She was not only beautiful, as he'd discovered this morning before he knew who she was, but she was also well above average in intelligence and shared many of his interests. They were both trained in medicine, but they also shared a love of country-and-western music, mystery novels and the Oakland A's.

There was one thing he'd been right about this morning, however. She was one sexy lady! Not flashy or blatant. She did nothing to call attention to herself, but there was a warmth about her, a radiant appeal that drew him like a magnet and made him itch to touch her, hold her as he had for a few moments that morning when she had literally fallen into his arms, and caress the soft curves of her high breasts, small waist and enticing hips.

A wave of heat rolled through him and brought him back to reality with a thud. Damn! What was the matter with him? He was behaving more like a lusty teenager than an analytical physician who knew exactly what he did and didn't want in his life.

He definitely did not want Kirsten Reinhold! She would be a surefire impediment to his peace of mind.

Coralie and Jim were describing their wedding to Kirsten, and Sam jumped into the conversation at the first opportunity. "Coralie was so disappointed when you were unable to be maid of honor," he told Kirsten. "She said you were ill."

Kirsten nodded. "Yes, I was. It started with flulike symptoms that I couldn't seem to shake. I kept on working until one day I could hardly crawl out of bed, and then I went to the doctor. By that time it had gone into pneumonia, complicated by attacks of asthma. I was in and out of the hospital for more than a month.''

Concern and impatience warred in Sam as she talked. "Good Lord, woman," he growled. "You're a nurse. You must have known better than to ignore an illness that severe.''

He saw an answering impatience in her snapping brown eyes. "You're right, Doctor, but tell me something. How long does it take you to seek medical advice when you're sick?''

She had him there. "It doesn't apply to me. I'm a physician," he said evasively. "I can diagnose my own illnesses. Besides, I'm never sick.''

"Neither am I," she drawled, "and as a nurse I recognized the symptoms of viral influenza, but in the beginning they are also symptoms of a bad cold, and that's what I thought I had. By the time I realized it was more serious, I had pneumonia along with it.''

He frowned. "And the asthma? Is it chronic?''

She shook her head. "I never had it before in my life. At least, not that I know of. My doctor says I probably did, but like this time always thought it was a cold. Anyway, I had to take two courses of antibiotics to clear up the pneumonia, and steroids for the asthma.''

He wished she wouldn't bait him to anger and then make him feel like a brute when he responded. "And did they clear up the pneumonia and the asthma? Are you well now?''

She nodded, but still kept her eyes downcast. "Yes.''

He had an overwhelming desire to put his fingers under her chin and lift her face so she would have to look at him, but he didn't trust himself to touch her. "Then your doctor has given you a clean bill of health?''

Apparently she was going to make him pull the information out of her a word or sentence at a time.

"Not quite.'' She spoke in little more than a whisper.

"My immune system has been weakened, and he won't give me an okay to go back to work until next month."

Relief washed through Sam, and he tried for a lighter tone. "You have a smart physician. No doubt he told you to get plenty of rest and not to exert yourself?"

She did look up at him then and smiled. "Well, not exactly. What he said was to absorb plenty of sunshine and fresh air, but Eureka is on the ocean and the climate is damp and chilly most of the time—even in the summer. Coralie and Jim offered me the use of Jim's dad's house while he's gone, so I'm looking forward to breaking some horses and plowing the back forty."

She laughed and everyone laughed with her, but Sam wasn't altogether sure she was teasing.

Although the company was great and the conversation stimulating, by ten o'clock Sam was bone weary. It had been a long, busy, emotion-filled day, and if by some miracle he wasn't wakened during the night by a phone call he still had early appointments in the morning.

Besides, he could see that Kirsten was as exhausted as he. She'd only arrived this morning from California, which meant that she must have been on the road for the better part of three days. He would bet his practice her doctor hadn't approved that trip!

At the next break in the conversation he stifled a yawn and stood up. "I hate to break up the evening," he said with real regret, "but if you'll excuse me I'm going home to try for a couple of hours' sleep before someone else's cow has an obstetrical emergency."

They all laughed and stood up, too. "It's past my bed-time, also," Kirsten said. She was standing next to him, so close that the back of his hand brushed her skirt and sent tingles up his spine. "I'll help you with the dishes," she said to Coralie, "and then I'm going to the cottage."

"You'll do no such thing," Coralie admonished. "The girls have already cleared the table. All I have to do is stack the dishwasher, but since you left your car at Buck's and walked over, I'll drive you back to his house first. You do look tired.''

''I'll drop her off,'' Sam offered. After all, it was the polite thing to do, so why did his instinct warn him to shut up and leave? Let someone else take this cuddly kitten to her bedroom. He didn't want her sharp, little claws digging into him.

''That's not necessary,'' Kirsten protested. ''It's only about a block away. I can walk—''

''No you can't, city girl,'' Sam said, totally ignoring his better sense. ''You're not in town now. There are no street-lights, and you can't wander around a strange rural area in the dark.'' He eyed her feet. ''Especially not in those high heels.''

She knew he was right and didn't resist when he took her arm and turned them toward the door. ''I'll deliver you to your house. I don't want to be called out in the middle of the night to set your broken bones after a fall on this rough terrain.''

After friendly good-nights and thank-yous, Sam put Kirsten in his damaged car and within seconds they arrived at her destination. He shut off the motor and escorted her up to the house in the dark.

Kirsten was having second thoughts about her earlier attitude toward him. They'd both been rattled by the collision and had lashed out at each other in anger, without either giving the other the benefit of the doubt.

Since Sam and Jim were almost as close as brothers, she knew it would cause a lot of tension and dissension if she and Sam spent the next month sniping at each other. It was time for them to have a private talk and try to banish their animosity toward one another.

''Would you like to come in for a cup of coffee?'' she asked as she inserted her key in the lock.

Sam was surprised by the invitation. Her voice was low

and husky, and the wave of heat he'd felt earlier returned in force.

Would he? Damn right he would! And so would any other hot-blooded man she issued the invitation to. Was she coming on to him? Had she decided to play along with Coralie's matchmaking scheme for them after all?

No, he couldn't believe that. She seemed rather naive. She probably didn't realize what a late-night invitation like that so often implied. "Thank you, but may I take a rain check? You need your rest, and so do I."

That was a laugh. She'd just blown any thoughts of sleep out of the water for him.

The moon was bright enough that he could see her expression. She looked neither surprised nor disappointed as she opened the door. Instead she cleared her throat and said, "I noticed that Mr. Buckley's well-stocked cupboards include coffee, tea and cookies," she said flirtatiously.

Damn it, she *was* coming on to him. His stomach muscles clenched in a combination of interest and anger. He hadn't been so wrong about her this morning after all. Apparently she was going to play Coralie's game and look for a husband while she was here.

Well, he wasn't going to be titillated into marriage by any woman. "Kirsten, we have to talk." He tried to keep the anger out of his tone, but he wasn't succeeding.

He could see that she looked pleased. "All right, but let's go inside. We'd be more comfortable in the house than standing out here on the doorstep."

He sighed. She obviously wasn't going to make this easy for him. She must know that she had the power to convince him she was innocent of any wrongdoing even as she seduced him, and apparently she intended to use it. Fortunately, he wasn't as gullible as she thought.

"I'm sure we would be," he grated. "It would also make it easier for you to entice me into believing anything you wanted me to, but you might as well give up. I have no interest in getting married, either now or in the future."

This time she did react, and he had to give her credit for being a skilled actress. She truly looked dismayed and uncomprehending. "I don't—" she exclaimed, but he cut her off.

"Please, Kirsten, I know all about Coralie's plan to get you and me together. She thinks everyone has to be married to be truly happy, and since she found her true love through a personal ad she's decided to help you in your quest for a husband by being your matrimonial agent. What I can't figure out is why you'd go along with it. It's hard to believe that you can't find a husband on your own."

She gasped and blinked those expressive brown eyes. "I'm not looking for a husband," she protested vehemently. "And if I were I wouldn't need anyone's help finding one. I'm aware of what she's up to, and I've told her I'm not interested, but if you knew Coralie as well as you think you do you'd know that she's not easily dissuaded. She has only the best of intentions and I don't like to be rude, so I just let her prattle on and ignore all her well-meant advice."

She sounded so indignantly sincere that his first impulse was to back down and apologize, but that was exactly what she wanted. She even fluttered her long, thick eyelashes to make him think she was blinking back tears.

He drew a deep breath and hardened his resolve. "You're good. You really are," he said. "For a while there tonight you actually had me believing that you were as resistant to the interference as I am, but then you made the mistake of trying to seduce me."

He saw the flush of heat that turned her face red, but he was too late to deflect the full cutting force of her rage. "Why you arrogant bastard!" Her voice was low and filled with scorn. "Since when does an invitation to come in for coffee after a pleasant evening translate into a roll between the sheets? If that's been your experience, then the women around here must be awfully hard up for a man.''

Sam winced. It was obvious that he'd made another horrendous mistake in judgment, but she wasn't about to let him explain and apologize.

She turned toward the open door. ''I won't tell Jim about this because I don't want to cause any trouble between you, but I'm going to tell Coralie in no uncertain terms that I don't like you and do not want her to pair us together again. I'll make every effort to see to it that we don't run into each other for the duration of my stay here, and I expect you to do the same.''

She walked into the house and slammed the door behind her.

Chapter Three

Kirsten was wakened the following morning by a loud, piercing noise that brought her to a sitting position before she even had her eyes open.

What on earth was that? She blinked to chase away the sleep-induced fog and looked at her watch. Five o'clock! What was waking her up so early? It was barely light out.

The combination screech and yodel sounded again, but this time she recognized it as the crow of a rooster. She ran her fingers through her hair and snuggled back down into the comfortable double bed in the guest room of Buck Buckley's house.

It was a nice room, small but clean and starkly furnished in strictly male decor. A brass lamp and a serviceable alarm clock sat on the bedside chest, and a large framed print of a Remington cowboy scene hung on the dark wood wall above the bed. Directly across the room was a double chest of drawers with a wide mirror.

Kirsten sighed and closed her eyes again as the rooster continued to crow. She'd been exhausted when she went to bed the night before, but also too wrought up to sleep.

Damn Sam Lawford anyway! He'd had her totally off balance ever since their cars had collided. He'd made her feel alternately scared, guilty, anxious, angry, sorry and incompetent, and that was just in the half hour they'd spent together right after the accident.

She'd managed to calm down after arriving at the Buckley home, seeing her dear friend, Coralie, again and being welcomed into the bosom of her family. It had been so exciting that she'd even forgotten to report the accident to her insurance company, but then Dr. Sam had shown up and set her off again.

The man seemed to know exactly which buttons to push to scramble her wits! They'd finally gotten that confrontation untangled and were making friendly conversation and getting acquainted when he'd delivered her to her door and dropped that final bombshell.

Kirsten groaned and turned on her stomach to bury her face in the pillow and try to shut out the memory. Never had she been so mortified, or so furious, all at the same time. She wouldn't have believed there was room in her 125-pound body to contain such a storm of emotion.

How could he have misunderstood her friendly overture so completely? All she'd intended was to have a quiet chat over a cup of coffee, so they could iron out any remaining wrinkles in their ill-fated friendship. She'd figured she owed him that much since she was guilty of damaging his expensive car. What had she said or done to make him think she was trying to seduce him?

Either he was an egomaniac or an idiot, and she suspected it was both!

Rolling onto her back again she stretched both arms over her head. She'd been so upset when she went to bed the previous night that she hadn't been able to sleep. Instead she'd tossed and turned for an hour or so, then got up and rummaged through Buck's bookcase for something to read. She'd had a choice of mystery or western, and since she'd already read all the mysteries on Buck's shelves she settled for a shoot-'em-up western novel and read until one o'clock before her eyelids got heavy and began to close.

Now that pesky rooster was letting her know that it was time for any self-respecting farmer to be up and about. That apparently also included his wife, his children and any guests who might be lurking about. With a sigh she pushed aside the covers and more or less tumbled out of bed.

She had to have a private chat with Coralie, ASAP.

At about the same time six miles away in Copper Canyon, Sam rolled over in bed and shut off the blaring alarm clock. He was sorely tempted to lie back down and rest for just a few minutes before he got up, but he knew better than to do that.

After making a jackass of himself the previous night and insulting Kirsten, he'd tossed and turned for hours before finally falling asleep. Now he felt like a horse who'd been "rode hard and put away wet." If he dozed off he would oversleep, and then he would be running to catch up with his schedule all day and into the night.

With a moan he forced himself out of bed and stumbled into the bathroom. Years earlier when he was an intern he'd learned to brush his teeth, shave and dress while still half-asleep, and now it was more or less routine.

As he guided the electric razor over his bristly face his mind returned to the debacle with Kirsten the night before. He felt like a fool, which wasn't surprising because he *was* a fool. Why else would he have been so quick to jump to the conclusion that she was trying to get him into bed when all she'd offered was coffee and cookies?

The question was rhetorical because he already knew the answer. It was her voice. That low, sexy pitch that sent shivers down his spine. That was a come-on. It had to be.

Then again she'd cleared her throat directly after she'd spoken, and she'd recently been dangerously ill with a viral infection that could easily have affected her pharynx. Her voice could have been husky because the night air still impaired her vocal quality.

He slapped the heel of his hand against his forehead and glared at himself in the mirror.

Idiot! How come that thought just occurred to you? You're a doctor. You're supposed to be the expert on such things. Why didn't you figure that out last night before you opened your mouth and stuffed your foot in it?

His shoulders slumped and he turned off the razor as he muttered a barnyard oath. What was the matter with him? Why did he talk like a braying ass every time he tried to carry on a conversation with her? Nobody liked to be embarrassed by a slip of the tongue, but his tongue didn't just slip when he talked to Kirsten. It pitched and bucked and landed him flat on his backside.

Even more important, why did it matter so much to him? He didn't even know her. All told they'd only been together four and a half or five hours at the most. She was nothing to him but a damn nuisance, and still he felt sick when he remembered the pain and contempt in her tone as she'd delivered that last scathing and well-deserved tongue-lashing to him.

No woman since Belinda had been able to hurt and upset him so deeply, and that terrified him more than anything else that had happened. He'd vowed never to set himself up for that much agony again, and up to now he'd never allowed a woman to get close enough to try. It was obvious to him that he couldn't handle a busy medical practice and a deeply committed love affair at the same time. It had to be one or the other, and he had to make a living. Besides, his medical practice could never betray him the way a lover could.

Still, he had to apologize to Kirsten. He could never square it with his conscience if he didn't. As soon as he had a few minutes free he would call her, tell her how sorry he was for insulting her and try to persuade her to have dinner with him as a parting gesture. A way to try to soften some of the justifiable contempt she felt for him.

For some reason it was important to him that she not always remember him as an insensitive clod.

By eight o'clock breakfast had been served at the Buckley farm, and Jim and the hired man who was replacing Buck while he was gone had left to do whatever it was they did in the fields. Amber and Gloria were still asleep, and Coralie and Kirsten were taking a breather and having a second cup of coffee at the table in the kitchen.

Kirsten wanted to talk to Coralie about Sam, but she hoped to lead up to it gradually, instead of tackling the thorny subject head-on. The problem was she couldn't think of a way to do that, so she just asked the first question that came to mind. "What time do your stepdaughters wake up?"

Coralie chuckled. "During the school year they have to get up when Jim and I do, so we negotiated a compromise for the summer vacation. I've assigned each of them chores around the house that must be completed every day, but as long as they keep up with them I let them sleep as late as they want to in the mornings. So far it's working out beautifully."

Kirsten was surprised. "How did you get so knowledgeable about handling teenagers? As I remember from your letters, they were pretty undisciplined when you first came here."

Coralie shuddered. "That's an understatement, but I just think back to when I was their age and remember how I felt. Besides, they're at a time in life when their bodies are growing and changing so fast that they need a lot of sleep.

"Jim's daughters are very bright and mature. They're always open to suggestions, it's only orders they resist. But, hey, we've got much more exciting things to talk about than adolescent discipline.'' Her eyes twinkled, and a happy smile lit her face. "I'm dying to know how you liked Sam. Did you let him kiss you good-night when he took you home?''

Kirsten sighed and took a big swallow of her coffee. She'd known Coralie would be hoping to hear that Kirsten and Sam had fallen in love at first sight, and preferably that they'd already started making wedding plans.

She hated to dash Coralie's dream of negotiating a match made in heaven. Actually, now that there was no longer even the remotest possibility of such a thing happening, Kirsten realized that deep down she'd been more open to the idea than she'd been willing to admit, even to herself. It could have been great to live in a small country village as the wife of the town's handsome doctor.

But not this town's doctor! No way! Obviously Coralie didn't know that Jim's friend was a self-centered egotist who assumed that every woman he dated was panting to get him into bed.

Just thinking about it started her adrenaline pumping and gave her the energy to tackle the sensitive subject. "Coralie, we need to talk,'' she said carefully.

"I know. So talk,'' Coralie answered eagerly. "What did you think of him? Isn't he a hunk?''

"Oh, he's a hunk, all right,'' Kirsten agreed.

"Did he ask you to go out with him?'' Coralie obviously hadn't caught the sarcasm in Kirsten's tone.

"No, he didn't, and if he had I'd have said no,'' she answered starkly. Apparently there was no polite way she could make Coralie understand that her matchmaking was unwelcome, and Kirsten was through pussyfooting around.

Coralie's eyes widened. "But why? Are you two still upset over that accident? Surely you can put that behind you—''

"No, it's not that,'' Kirsten interrupted. "I'm sorry but I just don't like the man and he doesn't like me, either.''

Coralie looked stunned. "But I don't understand. You're both such nice people. How could you not like each other? What happened—"

Kirsten watched as her friend stopped in midsentence and her expression turned from puzzlement to shock. "Kirsten, he didn't try to—"

"No!" Oh Lord, this conversation was getting totally out of hand. She couldn't let Coralie think Sam had gotten rough or physical with her. "No, Coralie, he didn't try anything. He never laid a hand on me. Actually, sex is the last thing he'd want of me. I don't turn him on, that's for sure."

Coralie shook her head in disbelief, but Kirsten hurried on. "We did quarrel, but it was strictly verbal. Like I told you, we're just not compatible, and I'm afraid I have to insist that you forget about the matchmaking. Not only with Sam but with any man. I came here to visit you and your new family, not to find a husband. Please, honor my wishes."

"Well, of...of course I will if that's what you want." Coralie sounded dazed. "I'm so sorry—" Her sentence was cut short by the sound of feet clopping down the stairs just before Amber bounded into the room.

"Good morning," she said cheerfully. "Any chance of getting some breakfast?"

Coralie shut her mouth but seemed unable to shift her mind's gears onto a different subject, so Kirsten managed a big smile and answered for her. "You bet. The scrambled eggs and bacon are still warm on the back of the stove, and Coralie made the most mouth-watering banana muffins."

She pushed back her chair and stood up. "Sit down and I'll fix you a plate."

Amber waved her away and giggled. "Thanks, but we have rules around here. Anyone who's not at the table when meals are served has to wait on themselves."

Kirsten held up her hands in mock surrender. "Sorry. I

wouldn't dream of breaking any of the rules, so if you'll all excuse me I'll go back to my quarters and finish settling in."

She started walking toward the back door, when Coralie's voice stopped her. "Kirsten, I'll be finished up here in about an hour and then I'll come over. I want to talk to you. We have a lot to catch up on."

Kirsten got the message. "Great. Bring a couple of those muffins and I'll put the teakettle on."

It was nearly ten o'clock when Coralie tapped on the door to Buck's little house. Kirsten had spent the intervening time pacing the floor, berating herself for being so outspoken about her dislike for Sam and wondering if she'd done irreparable harm to her treasured friendship with Coralie.

She hurried to open the door and admit her friend. "You don't have to knock," she said. "After all, this is your house."

Coralie stepped inside. "It may be owned by the family corporation," she acknowledged, "but it's the home of whomever happens to be in residence at the time, and right now that's you. I wouldn't violate your privacy by just walking in."

Kirsten uttered a wry, little laugh. "Believe me, my life's an open book—or door as the case may be. Shall we sit over here on the sofa?"

They walked across the living room and sat down on the brown velour couch. There was also a rust-colored lounge chair and a deep leather easy chair, as well as a console television set and assorted small tables. A brick fireplace dominated the side wall, and a picture window took up most of the front one.

Coralie crossed one jeans-clad leg over the other and tried to appear relaxed, but the nervous twisting of her hands gave away her unease. Kirsten, also wearing jeans, had taken off her shoes and tucked her feet beneath her.

Coralie was the first to speak. "I...I've been thinking about our earlier conversation, and I'm so sorry if my good intentions seemed more like meddling—"

"No, Coralie, please," Kirsten interrupted. "It wasn't like that at all. It's just that neither Sam nor I are ready for a long-term relationship with anybody. Even if we were, it wouldn't be with each other. The chemistry's just not right between us."

Coralie looked thoughtful. "It's not just you. It would have been that way with any woman I tried to fix Sam up with. I should have known better than to interfere in his hermitlike existence."

Kirsten regretted that she'd made her friend feel guilty. All Coralie had done was introduce a man and a woman who were good friends of hers, and whom she was sure would be compatible.

"Don't blame yourself," Kirsten said gently. "You had no way of knowing Sam and I would be so antagonistic toward each other."

Coralie shook her head. "That's just it. I should have known. As I said before, it's not you personally that he dislikes, it's the fact that you're a woman."

Kirsten gasped. "You mean he doesn't like women! But why would you—?"

Coralie looked as startled as Kirsten felt. "No, no, I didn't mean that," she hastened to say. "He likes women, but the one he fell in love with betrayed him and broke his heart."

Kirsten sank back against the sofa. "Oh," she exclaimed on a sigh. "You mean he's divorced?"

"No, they'd been engaged for several years, but were waiting until he finished his internship before getting married."

Kirsten found that hard to fathom. "But why—"

Coralie made a face. "Don't ask me. Still, it's not as if they were celibate all that time. They lived together while he was in medical school."

Kirsten made a gesture of frustration. "I've never understood cohabitation. When a couple lives together, they make a strong commitment to each other whether they realize it at the time or not. They have most of the obligations of marriage but none of the legal protection, so why not take the vows?"

Coralie chuckled. "Hey, Ms. Old-Fashioned Gal, come on down off your soapbox. I've heard your fiery rhetoric before. In fact, as I remember, it was aimed at me once."

"Yes, and you took my advice. If you'll remember, you thanked me for it later. Said I'd saved you from making a big mistake." Kirsten looked away, embarrassed. "Sorry. I didn't mean to preach. I just hate to see any woman allow herself to be put in a vulnerable position."

"Well, don't worry about Belinda," Coralie said emphatically. "She was the one who broke it off and took Sam for everything she could. I don't have all the details. He never talks about it, so all I know is what Jim's told me and what I've learned from gossip the local citizens were eager to impart. In a small town like Copper Canyon everybody knows everybody else's business."

Kirsten's curiosity was nagging at her. "Well, for heaven's sake," she said impatiently, "what happened?"

"It's a long story," Coralie began. "Her name was Belinda Evans, and her and Sam's parents were close friends, so they'd known each other all their lives. They'd been best friends in elementary and middle school, sweethearts in high school and lovers in college. I gather that it wasn't until his last year in medical school that the trouble between them erupted."

"But if they were so much in love, why didn't they get married?" Kirsten repeated.

Coralie rolled her eyes. "I told you, I don't know. You

know how college kids are. They like to be independent. Maybe Sam and Belinda were rebelling against authority, or maybe they wanted to make a statement. Who knows. I asked Jim one time and he said he didn't know and hadn't asked, implying that it was none of anybody else's business."

Kirsten smiled sheepishly. "Yeah. Well, I have to admit he's right... So go ahead. What happened to break them up?"

"When Sam started medical school in Chicago, Belinda went along with him and they set up housekeeping together. The idea was for her to work and help support them, but her college degree was in humanities, which didn't qualify her for much of anything unless she did graduate work. She had trouble finding a job, and when she did find one it was as an entry-level salesperson in a department store at only slightly above minimum wage."

Kirsten was puzzled. "I understood Sam's father was a physician. Couldn't he pay for his son's schooling?"

"Well, yes, he could and did," Coralie explained, "but physicians in small communities aren't as well paid as those in the cities, and the tuition to medical school is terribly expensive. Sam didn't want to burden him with Belinda's living expenses, too. After all, there were other children in the family who had to be educated."

"Yes, I see," Kirsten said. "Was it their financial problems that caused Sam and Belinda to break up?"

Coralie frowned. "No, actually it was the long hours of work and study his training required that finally did them in. She was lonely, irritable and desperately unhappy, when so many of his nights as well as his days were spent at the hospital.

"He tried to explain to her that this was the type of thing all medical students went through and there was nothing he could do about it, but by then she was beyond reason and started accusing him of seeing another woman."

"She didn't!" Kirsten protested. "Students always work gruelingly long hours in medical school and during their internship, to say nothing of residency if they decide to specialize."

Coralie shrugged. "Not everyone knows that," she pointed out. "You and I do because we also studied in the medical field, but Belinda had no such frame of reference. Her dad's a blue-collar worker who got excellent technical training in an apprenticeship program but never went to college. She got a degree, but chose easy courses and only studied hard enough to get by. According to Jim, she didn't really want to work. She wanted to marry a wealthy man who would support her."

"Lazy, wasn't she," Kirsten muttered through tight lips. She'd heard enough to thoroughly dislike this woman.

"Afraid so," Coralie agreed, "but according to Jim nobody dared say that to Sam. Jim tried it once and nearly got his head taken off. Sam was blindly in love and couldn't or wouldn't see her faults."

"So what finally happened?" Kirsten prodded again.

Coralie's tone and expression deepened to sadness. "Sam came home to their apartment one night to find Belinda gone. She'd taken all her things with her and left a note saying she couldn't live the way they were any longer."

Coralie's voice broke. "He had some critically important exams coming up in the next few days and couldn't take time off to track her down and beg her to come back. By the time he found her a couple of weeks later she'd married a man who, he learned belatedly, had been keeping her company during the long hours when Sam was at the hospital."

A surge of compassion for Sam temporarily displaced the anger Kirsten had been feeling. "What a rotten thing for a woman to do to a man!" she said indignantly. "He must have been devastated."

"He was," Coralie confirmed, "and he never got over it. Oh, he doesn't dwell on it, but neither has he had anything but superficial relationships with any woman since. That's why I was so eager to get you and him together. You're so right for each other, but obviously he wants no part of it."

Kirsten's tender heart hurt for Sam, who had been so badly treated by this spoiled and selfish woman. She wished she could hold him, comfort him, take away the lingering pain, but that was her nurturing instinct reacting, not her good sense.

In fact, it was all the more reason for her to steer clear of him. She was too vulnerable to him, too empathetic to his anguish, and she sure didn't want to get mixed up in that quagmire!

"You can't blame him, can you?" Kirsten said. "He might never completely trust a woman again. I wish I could help him, but I can't. Nobody can, until he admits he needs it and asks for it."

She paused for a moment and softened her tone. "And, Coralie, you're not doing the women you set him up with any favor by trying to interest him in another relationship. He'll just drive them away like he did me."

Coralie opened her mouth to say something, but Kirsten hurried on. "This is a problem he needs to work out on his own or with a counselor. You know that. We both had lots of psychology classes in college. Enough to know when we can help with a patient's emotional problems and when we can't."

Finally Coralie got a word in edgewise. "As you said, I know all that, and I certainly wouldn't try to involve him with just any woman, but you're special and I have this gut feeling that you're the one who can restore his belief in the female gender and teach him to love again."

Coralie's statement pushed the wrong button in Kirsten. "That's nonsense!" she railed. "And besides, I don't want to have to 'teach' a man to love me. If my future Mr. Right can't fall in love with me without help, then I don't need him."

She realized she sounded strident and lowered her voice. "I don't want warmed-over love, Coralie. That's a surefire road to hell. I want a man who will cherish me because he can't help himself. Who will marry me because he can't imagine life without me. Not one who thinks of another woman every time he makes love with me."

Chapter Four

Kirsten spent the remainder of the morning on the phone reporting the accident to her insurance company in California, then helping Coralie prepare dinner, which in the rural areas of Idaho was the big meal served at noon. According to Coralie, it always consisted of meat, potatoes, gravy, vegetables, salad, bread and butter and dessert. The night meal was a smaller one called supper, as Kirsten had found out yesterday.

Jim and the hired man, Will Tucker, came in promptly at noon, washed up, ate ravenously and then Will went back to work while Coralie and Jim disappeared upstairs for a little while. Not long enough for any serious lovemaking, but when they came back down they looked flushed and happy.

They obviously adored each other, and Kirsten felt a twinge of envy. Was there a man out there somewhere who would love her as much as Jim loved Coralie? She hoped so, but that kind of devotion was rare and precious.

Not many people were blessed with a soul mate.

By two o'clock Coralie and Kirsten had finished cleaning

up the kitchen, and Kirsten was exhausted. She'd gotten up with the rooster at five, and the hours since had been busy and exciting, but tiring. She hadn't quite realized how thoroughly her energy had been drained by her illness, and even though she'd followed her doctor's orders and taken it reasonably easy driving from Eureka, the two and a half days on the road had been debilitating.

She excused herself to go back to the cottage and take a nap. Coralie not only agreed, but insisted that she rest until suppertime, which was just fine with Kirsten. She was asleep within minutes after she stretched out on the bed, and didn't wake up until the phone rang nearly three hours later.

It was almost as jarring as the rooster had been, and she woke with a start. "Hello," she mumbled fuzzily into the speaker.

"Kirsten?" It was a man's voice and sounded vaguely familiar. "This is Sam Lawford. Did I wake you?"

Sam? Why on earth would he be calling her? She'd been under the impression that they had said a very unmistakable and permanent goodbye last night.

"What is it you want, Sam?" she snapped, still groggy from sleeping so soundly. "Yes, you did wake me, but that's all right. If I'd slept any longer, I'd have had trouble sleeping tonight."

"I'm sorry. I didn't mean to disturb you," he said. "I called for you earlier at the big house, and Coralie said you were taking a nap at Buck's and not to wake you. I thought you'd be up by now. Are you all right?" He sounded as if he actually cared, which just showed how confused she was.

"I'm fine," she said grumpily, wishing he would leave her alone.

"Are you still taking medication?"

"No, just vitamins. Look, Sam, I think I made my feelings plain last night. I don't have anything more to say to you—"

"I'm glad of that," he said with feigned relief. "You about seared the hide off me the last time we spoke."

"You deserved it," she said emphatically.

"I know I did." His tone was contrite. "That's why I'm calling. You didn't give me a chance to say anything before you slammed the door in my face. I was awake most of the night regretting my hasty assumptions—"

"Yes, well, I'm really not interested," she said, interrupting him. "Now, if you'll excuse me—"

"No, don't hang up," he said urgently. "Please, at least give me a chance to apologize—"

"Why?"

"Wh-what do you mean, why?"

She grimaced. "Why do you want to apologize? You sure didn't have any doubts last night when you were making all those insulting accusations, so why is it important now that you ask for forgiveness?"

A thought occurred to her. "If you're worried about what Jim and Coralie will think of you, don't. I didn't tell them what happened. I just told Coralie that we don't like each other and want her to stop with the matchmaking."

"I wasn't even thinking about Jim and Coralie's opinion of my boorish behavior. It's your impression of me I'm hoping to change," he admitted. "I agree that there's no excuse for the way I acted, but I am deeply sorry and I'd like the chance to try to make amends by taking you to dinner tonight someplace quiet where we can talk."

Her stomach muscles tightened with outrage at his apparent assumption that all he had to do was turn on the charm, feed her a little humble pie along with a meal and she would immediately forgive him anything.

"No, Sam," she said coldly. "I'm sorry you have so much trouble accepting rejection, but I meant every word

I said to you last night. I don't want to see or hear from you again."

She put the phone back into its cradle and noticed that her hands were shaking. She hated it that he still had the power to upset her so badly.

Sam hung up his office phone and sighed. Well, he'd tried. Kirsten had certainly made her feelings plain, so there was really nothing else he could do without becoming a pest. He could send her flowers with a note of apology, but she would no doubt just throw them out.

He ran his hands through his hair, then stretched his arms to try to loosen the knotted muscles in his neck and shoulders. He was tired and had the beginnings of a headache from sleeping so poorly the previous night.

Why was this woman playing such havoc with his peace of mind? True, he'd behaved badly toward her, but even that was uncharacteristic. His mother had been very insistent on teaching her two sons and two daughters to be polite at all times. So much so, that Sam usually found it difficult to speak harshly to anybody, even someone who deserved it.

So why did he verbally attack Kirsten every time they spoke? His rage over the damage to his car was understandable, but he'd overreacted. After all she hadn't hit him on purpose, and she'd apologized and assured him her insurance would cover the cost of repairs. Still, he'd felt...threatened? That was the only word that came to mind. After he'd ascertained that she wasn't injured, she'd looked at him with those big, expressive eyes that mirrored both confusion and regret, and a slow warmth had stolen over him, melting the defenses he'd so carefully built up after Belinda—

He pushed back his chair and stood. No, he wasn't going to think of Belinda! He'd gotten over her. Sometimes weeks went by without her image filling his mind, the sound of her low, breathless voice whispering risqué suggestions in his ears or the memory of the touch of her soft, little hands caressing him.

Belinda, his childhood playmate, his best friend, his lover and intended wife, had betrayed him in the most painful way possible, and he'd vowed never to let a woman close enough to cause him so much anguish ever again.

Could it be that Kirsten reminded him of her? He shook his head in silent denial. Possible, but not likely. Physically, Belinda was tiny, five feet tall at the most and weighing maybe ninety-five pounds, with long blond hair and blue eyes; whereas, Kirsten was five-six or so with a larger frame, although it was beautifully shaped. She had short, dark, curly hair and brown eyes.

No, his antagonism toward Kirsten had nothing to do with Belinda. It was probably just the shock of the collision and finding that the luxury car he'd finally acquired after years of dreaming about it had been mangled on one side.

He was truly sorry he'd acted like such a jerk to her and he wanted to make it up in some way, but apparently that wasn't possible. She wouldn't listen to his apology, and she refused to see him again or accept anything from him. The only thing left was to leave her alone as she'd requested.

In Kirsten's mind the next week went by in a whirl of sight-seeing and meeting new people. Coralie took her on a tour of Copper Canyon, a village of approximately three thousand souls. It was picturesque, with plenty of shade trees and colorful flower gardens in the residential area, and a main street with all the necessary businesses to make the town self-sufficient and reasonably solvent.

They also cruised the surrounding area, mostly historical Nez Percé Indian land. They explored the Camas Prairie, where the Native Americans once dug camas root to supplement their diet; the White Bird battlefield, sight of the first confrontation of the Nez Percé War; and Orofino, a small town on the nearby reservation that was one of Idaho's first permanent settlements.

She'd met a number of the townspeople. George White, the butcher, who also owned the town's version of a supermarket; Walter Sutter, pharmacist and owner of Sutter's Drugstore; and Butch Jackson, the "son" of Jackson and Son's Garage, where Kirsten had taken her car to have the dents ironed out.

Butch had heard all about the accident and told her Dr. Sam had brought his "Beemer" in for a checkup to make sure it was in good enough shape to drive to Boise.

"He wouldn't let me touch the bodywork," Butch complained. "Said he was taking it back to the dealer in Boise where they specialize in BMWs."

He snorted. "We don't see many luxury cars around here, but I can work on any make or model. Hell, I let him deliver my two kids, but he won't trust me to repair his fancy car?"

Kirsten felt a twinge of guilt again. She'd not only severely inconvenienced Sam, but she'd put him in a position of offending a patient's family.

Finally she'd met Copper Canyon's chief of police, when she and Coralie went to the station to report the accident as required by her insurance company. Richard McBride was a big man, well over six feet tall with chest, shoulder and arm muscles that rippled under his blue uniform shirt.

Coralie had told her that there wasn't much crime in the area, and Kirsten could see why. *She* would sure think twice before she tangled with this man, even though his smile was as sunny as his golden hair, and his demeanor was friendly and polite. He seemed young to be a police chief—Coralie said he was thirty—but he'd studied police science in college.

He'd asked her right then and there to go out with him, and impulsively she'd accepted. After all, he was a friend of the Buckleys and certainly respectable. And this date wasn't orchestrated by anyone but him, so she didn't feel pressured.

They'd had dinner and gone to a movie that night, and two days later he'd taken her for an all-day jet-boat excursion and picnic on the Salmon River near Riggins with two other couples. They'd boated past abandoned mines, old Native American fishing camps and burial grounds, and had thrilled at the sight of wild deer, elk and mountain goats.

It had been an exciting and fun-filled day, and the following morning one of the other two men on the excursion, Don Sterling, an insurance agent approximately her age, with red hair and freckles, called and invited her to a barbecue and swimming party on Wednesday evening at the home of his brother.

It was now Wednesday and less than an hour before Don was due to pick her up, and she still hadn't decided what to wear.

"Put on your bathing suit first," Coralie advised as they inspected the clothes in the closet of Kirsten's bedroom. "Then wear shorts and a shirt over it. They'll want to swim before they eat, and that way you'll only have to slip off the shorts and shirt and you'll be all ready to jump in the pool."

Kirsten rummaged through a dresser drawer and brought out a minuscule coral-spandex-threaded-with-gold bikini with a matching sheer rayon cover-up. "Excuse me a minute while I put this on," she said as she headed for the bathroom. "I want your opinion."

Quickly she put the suit on, then snatched the cover-up and carried it over her arm.

"Do you think this is too revealing for the citizens of Copper Canyon?" she asked timidly.

Coralie's eyes widened. "Wow!" she exclaimed. "Hey, sweetie, I don't think I want my Jim to see you in that.

You'd make any man's mouth water, and I don't want him thinking those thoughts about any woman but me.''

Kirsten slumped. "Then it *is* too skimpy. I bought it just before I left Eureka to come here, and I didn't take into account the difference between urban California and rural Idaho. I don't have another one.''

Coralie chuckled. "It's not too skimpy. You're just too damn well built. Go ahead and wear it. I was mostly teasing. You'd look sexy in any swimsuit you put on.''

Kirsten wasn't convinced. Then she remembered the cover-up. She shook it out and held it up. "How about this?'' she asked as she slipped her arms through the sleeveless armholes. It was a full trapeze-style cut and came to just below the top of her thighs.

Coralie whistled. "It's beautiful. The whole outfit is, but I have to tell you that transparent jacket doesn't hide any of your assets, although I can't imagine why you'd want it to.''

Coralie chuckled again, and Kirsten picked up a small throw pillow from the bed and tossed it at her. "Damn it, Coralie,'' she scolded. "Stop that. I'm serious. Shall I wear the suit or not?''

Coralie ducked, narrowly avoiding the pillow. "Well,'' she drawled as she looked Kirsten up and down, "I don't think you want to go swimming without it.''

At that they both broke into laughter, and Coralie picked up the pillow and threw it back at Kirsten.

"Oh, for heaven's sake wear it,'' Coralie said when they finally managed to stifle their giggles. "It's stunning and must have cost you a fortune.''

Kirsten knew why she hesitated. Sam Lawford's inference that she was a tease and a flirt had hurt worse than she'd wanted to admit. It had also rattled her self-confidence. If she came across that way to him, maybe other men formed that opinion also.

She'd always tried to behave like a lady, and it upset her to think that other people might think otherwise.

She couldn't tell that to Coralie, though. Instead, she said, "I wouldn't want to wear or do anything that might embarrass you and your family." That was also the truth.

Coralie stopped smiling. "Kirsten, there is nothing you would do that would make me ashamed of you. How could you ever think otherwise? Now, get into your shorts and shirt. Don will be here any minute."

Jeff and Nancy Sterling had a lovely home. Not terribly large, but new and tastefully decorated. The backyard was spacious and easily contained the pool, a small pool house and the patio.

Don told Kirsten that the two brothers, along with their father, owned a family insurance business called, not surprisingly, Sterling Insurance.

There were about ten people already there when Don and Kirsten arrived, and most of them were in the pool. There was a lot of yelling, splashing and laughing going on, and Don whistled, loud and clear, to get their attention.

"Hey, guys," he said, and put his arm around Kirsten. "I want you to meet my date, Kirsten Reinhold. She lives in California and is visiting Jim and Coralie Buckley. As soon as we get our suits on and join you in the pool, you can come up and introduce yourselves to her."

They all waved cheerfully and called hello, and Kirsten was relieved to note that hers wasn't the only skimpy bikini in sight. Still, when she stepped out of the pool house after taking off her shorts and shirt, all eyes turned toward her. She saw admiration and a touch of lust in the gazes of the men, and the women were lavish with their compliments and wanted to know where they could get a suit like it.

Don joined her, and for the next forty-five minutes they had a great time swimming and playing games in the pool. A few more people arrived and were introduced to Kirsten, and she heard talk of another guest who was late. "But that's nothing new," one of the women said. "He seldom gets anyplace on time. That man works too hard."

Someone threw a beach ball into the water, starting a game of catch that ended the conversation before Kirsten heard a name mentioned.

A few minutes later Don excused himself and got out of the pool to help his brother at the barbecue. She realized she was feeling chilled from being too long in the cold water, and knowing she was still vulnerable after her illness, she climbed out and stretched full length on a lounge chair in the warmth of the sun.

The sun in Idaho was brighter than in coastal northern California, where it was shrouded in fog or clouds, and in no time its heat had penetrated the chill and left her feeling drowsy.

In spite of the comfort, it annoyed her to once again be forced to admit that she still hadn't regained all her strength. Ordinarily she could play on the beach and swim in the rough, icy ocean waters back home without ever tiring, but now an hour in the sun-warmed water of a backyard pool exhausted her.

She'd always been healthy, seldom even had a cold until that nasty virus crept up on her, and she had no patience with her stubborn weakness.

Sam brought his gleaming, newly repaired white BMW to a screeching halt on the driveway of his two-story Victorian house, which had been the Lawford family home for over three generations. A glance at the modular clock on the dash told him it was almost seven o'clock. He was already an hour late for Jeff and Nancy's party, and he still had to shower and change clothes.

He rushed into the house, stripped and stood under the pounding warm water in the master bathroom. All day he'd been looking forward to a swim in the Sterlings' new pool, but now it was too late. He would be lucky if he made it in time for the buffet.

For most of the afternoon it had looked as though he might get out of the office on time, but then just as he was finishing with his last patient the hospital had called to tell him Tubby Smith's wife had brought him in again with severe angina pains.

Sam had no choice but to rush right over, as he had every other time this had happened. The man was his own worst enemy. He was almost one hundred pounds overweight, got practically no exercise, and had been smoking between two and three packs of cigarettes a day for the past thirty years. At the age of fifty-six he was headed for a massive coronary and there was nothing Sam could do about it as long as Tubby refused to exercise and give up the cigarettes and rich foods.

Remembering that he didn't have time to waste, Sam rinsed off the soapsuds, turned off the water and toweled himself dry. After a quick shave he dressed in light blue cotton shorts and a royal-blue-and-white sport shirt with splashes of red, then gathered up his swim trunks and a towel in the hope that some of the guests might want to swim again after they ate.

The big, old grandfather clock chimed the half hour as he strode out the door, slamming it behind him. Seven-thirty. Damn, he sure hoped there was some food left by the time he got there.

Kirsten realized she'd dozed off when a babble of excited voices greeting someone woke her. Apparently the guest who was late had just arrived. The aroma of barbecuing beef and chicken wafted toward her on the air, and she realized she was hungry. She was also still more asleep than awake, and she snuggled into the padded lounge and again closed her eyes. Maybe she could rest a little longer before supper was called. The happy sounds of the party receded as she drifted back into slumber....

She felt the hand on her shoulder just a second before the voice spoke. "Kirsten, wake up. The buffet's ready and it's time to eat."

It was a man's voice, and she blinked and opened her eyes expecting to see Don. Instead it was *Sam*. She blinked again, sure that she was struggling to wake up and her eyes were playing tricks on her.

They weren't. It was still Sam bending over her when she opened them again. He was sitting on the edge of the lounge with one hand on her shoulder, gently shaking her awake. He smiled and moved his hand to the side of her neck where it settled.

"Sam?" she said sleepily. "What are you doing here?"

"Trying to save you from a sunburn and interest you in some food." He spoke softly and rubbed one finger along her jaw. "If I haven't lost my diagnostic ability, I'd say you're not wearing sunscreen."

She raised her arm and looked at it. It was turning a very light pink. "Oh, my. I didn't even think... I was only going to lie here in the sun for a few minutes until I got warm."

His finger stopped its caressing and he frowned. "Were you having chills?"

Now he sounded like her doctor. "Only because I'd been in the water too long. Really, Sam, I'm not your patient."

The frown disappeared and his finger once more stroked her jaw. "No, you're not," he said apologetically. "But I worry about you all the same. I have some cream in the car that will keep that slight burn from turning painful."

He removed his hand and stood, and she noticed that he was wearing shorts. It was the first time she'd seen his bare legs, and the sight was a real treat. They were strong, muscular and well shaped, just like the rest of him. She had an urge to pull him back down again and keep him with her. Had he meant it when he said he worried about her?

"I'll go get it," he continued. "It won't take a minute. Don't put any more clothes on until I get back." He turned and walked away before she could protest.

While he was gone, Kirsten got up and moved the lounger into the shade. She noticed that the other guests were lining up at the buffet, and most of them had changed back into shorts, slacks and shirts. That was when it hit her that she was still wearing her revealing swimsuit, and Sam had seen her in it.

She groaned and sat back down. Would he hold her state of undress against her, too? She told herself it didn't matter, but she knew it did. He hadn't said anything about it, so maybe he hadn't noticed.

Quickly she reached for the short cover-up and was buttoning it down the front when he returned.

He handed her a small square box with the name of a pharmaceutical company printed on it. "Here. This cream is cool and soothing, and there are several sample tubes in there, so use it lavishly."

"Thank you," she said, and noticed that his smile had turned to a frown.

"I told you not to put any more clothes on," he reminded her. "How are we going to rub you down if you're all covered up?"

His phraseology sent a jolt of heat through her that was hotter than the sunburn, and she responded without taking time to think. "*We* aren't going to rub me down. *I am.* And I can manage very well, thank you."

He looked momentarily abashed, then grinned. "Oh, shucks," he drawled bashfully and hung his head. "And here I was so looking forward to the job."

Kirsten laughed. She couldn't help it. His shy country-boy act was so out of character.

He laughed, too, and the constraint between them was broken.

"I'm sorry," she said when she got her voice under control. "I keep forgetting you're a doctor. I didn't mean to imply—"

"Kirsten," he interrupted, his expression serious, "I'm still a man, and that bathing suit you're wearing is playing havoc with my professional detachment."

She looked down, embarrassed and disappointed. "You don't like it?"

Sam sat down beside her and ran his hand through his hair. "Of course I like it. I've never seen a prettier one, or one more beautifully displayed. You have a perfect body, and I'm sure you've been told before that you're a vision of sheer delight in anything you wear. Now, why don't you take off that shirt and let me apply cream to your back and arms while you concentrate on your chest, stomach and legs."

She found she liked that idea very much, and saw no reason why she shouldn't agree. After handing him the box to open, she unfastened the cover-up and slid it off her shoulders. He gave her one tube and then opened another.

Kirsten squeezed a liberal amount of cream into her hands and applied it to her chest and stomach, while Sam's talented hands gently rubbed the cooling substance into her back and shoulders.

"I didn't know you were going to be here today," he said. "Don says you're his date. I was late getting here, and he brought me over to introduce us, but you were resting so peacefully that I told him we'd already met and not to wake you until they were ready to eat. He's the one who sent me over to wake you up."

Kirsten felt a wave of guilt. Some date she was. She should have been helping Don with the food instead of falling asleep.

On the other hand Sam's touch was so soothing. It felt like a caress, and her muscles relaxed under his gentle massage and left her feeling limp and tension free. With only a slight pressure he maneuvered her backward so her bare upper back and shoulders leaned against his chest.

"I don't mean to sound like a grumpy, old doctor," he murmured in her ear as he stroked cream on her upper arms, "but you really must try to pace yourself better until you've regained your strength. The pneumonitis that was so prevalent last spring is a difficult strain. It's hard to treat and slow to cure. It might recur, and that could be extremely serious."

He really seemed concerned, and she realized she liked it. Maybe they had just gotten off to an unfortunate start, she reasoned. That didn't mean she shouldn't give him another chance. Not at a permanent relationship, of course. Neither of them wanted that, but it would be nice if they could get along for Jim and Coralie's sake.

Coralie had made so many plans for the four of them, and Kirsten and Sam's antagonism toward each other had really put a damper on them. Kirsten decided if Sam still wanted to apologize she would let him and hope they could be more compatible.

How could she help but forgive him when his hands were doing such pleasurable things to her? And without ever touching areas of her body that were considered off-limits in public.

"I...I'd better get dressed," she stammered as she finished rubbing the cream on her legs, then put the cap back on the tube. "And I'm afraid I owe Don an apology. I've never been so rude as to fall asleep at a party before."

Sam also capped his tube and put it back in the box, then handed the box to her. "Here. Put this with your things and take it home with you. Just tell Don you've been ill. He's a nice guy and will understand."

Then they went their separate ways, and once she was dressed Kirsten joined Don at the buffet table. "Don, I'm so sorry," she said contritely. "It was inexcusable of me to fall asleep."

He smiled at her. "Not at all. I'm the one who should apologize for leaving you alone so much of the time. Nancy had hired a couple of high-school girls to help with the food and at the last minute they backed out. Jeff asked if I could lend a hand for a little while, and you seemed to be having a good time in the pool so I agreed. I was about to break away when I noticed you were asleep, so…"

Kirsten chuckled. "I guess we're equally at fault, but I'm not upset if you're not."

He leaned down and kissed her on the forehead. "How could anyone be upset with you? Now, grab a plate and let's eat."

She and Sam weren't alone again for the rest of the evening.

Chapter Five

Sam was one of the first to leave the party, even though he'd arrived late. When saying goodbye to his hosts, he'd used the excuse that he had an early morning surgery scheduled for the next day.

That was true, but he hadn't mentioned that it was a routine tubal ligation that he could no doubt perform in his sleep. He'd needed a reason for leaving without appearing rude, and work was the first one that came to mind. He wasn't even sure why he was in such a tearing hurry to get away.

As he drove along the darkened streets he pondered that last thought. It wasn't true. He knew damn good and well why he'd wanted to leave. He just didn't want to admit it. Not even to himself.

He'd been surprised and overjoyed to find Kirsten at the party when he'd arrived, but then he learned she was with Don. He'd already heard of her date with the chief of police—gossip spread fast in a small town—and tonight he'd come face-to-face with yet another of her suitors. Did she plan to go through the whole roster of Copper Canyon's bachelors while she was here?

Well, that wouldn't be hard, he thought ruefully. There weren't all that many eligible young men around anymore. And there were even fewer unmarried young women. Instead the population was comprised mostly of families with children at one extreme and the elderly men and women who had been born and raised in Copper Canyon at the other. Over the past several years all those in between had left for college or jobs in urban areas after graduating from high school and they seldom came back.

Copper Canyon was a peaceful little town with a breathtaking view of rugged mountain peaks on one side and rolling hills of grain on the other, but it had little to offer its young people anymore. Most of the businesses were family owned and operated, and the nearest cities of any size were much too far away to commute.

So it was no wonder Kirsten was being wined and dined by a different man every other night. God knows, she was beautiful, smart and incredibly sexy. What male wouldn't want to take her out? Including himself!

Ah, yes, there was the problem. Apparently she was friendly, sociable and enjoyed dating every man who asked her out. Every one except him.

It shouldn't bother him, it was his own fault. But it did. It hurt to hear of her dates with other men, and it had been especially painful to watch her tonight with Don. Sam had thought he was making headway in his effort to convince her that he wasn't really as obnoxious as he'd appeared to be in their first two encounters. She'd even smiled at him and let him apply lotion to her sunburned back.

He shivered as he remembered the smooth, soft texture of her bare flesh under his palms. She was every bit as delightful to the touch as he'd imagined she would be. When she'd leaned back against him it was all he could do not to rub his cheek in her short tangle of dark curls and nibble on her slender neck.

But then Don beckoned and she'd taken off without a backward glance. Well, what had he expected? She was Don's guest.

With a massive effort he forced himself to cut off that line of thought. His reaction to her didn't mean a thing. She was a highly sensual woman and he was a normal warm-blooded male. It wasn't surprising that having her so close would arouse him. It would have been abnormal if it hadn't!

It couldn't be jealousy that gnawed at his insides, he told himself. It was just his ego that was bruised.

The following noon, dinner at the Buckley farm was just winding down with thick slices of homemade peach pie and fresh cream when the phone rang. Coralie jumped up and went into the kitchen to answer it, then returned a minute later with a happy grin. "It's for you, Kirsten," she said and slid back into her seat.

"Me?" Kirsten asked and pushed back her chair. "Who is it?"

Coralie didn't answer, but as Kirsten went past her she looked up, winked and said softly, "Now be nice, you hear?"

Kirsten frowned. What on earth did she mean by that? She was never knowingly unkind to anyone.

She picked up the receiver and said hello.

"Kirsten, this is Sam Lawford."

His voice was familiar to her now, and it sent pinpricks of surprise and—surely it couldn't be joy—down her spine. "Sam? Coralie said you want me?"

She spoke without thinking, then realized immediately that it could be taken in ways other than how she'd intended, but he just chuckled. "That's a loaded statement, but for now I only want to talk to you. How are you today?

Are you still tiring easy? Do you need more cream for your sunburn?"

He had the sexiest damn voice. Low and husky, with a hint of passion so subtle that she couldn't be sure if it was really there or if she just hoped it was.

"I—I'm fine," she stammered. "I feel well rested, and my sunburn is more tan than pink. It doesn't hurt at all. I still have plenty of medication, but thanks for taking the time to ask."

"I told you before, I worry about you," he said. "I'd like to get to know you better. You don't have something going with Don Sterling do you?"

"What do you mean by *something going?*" she asked huffily. She should have known he couldn't say more than a few sentences to her without insulting her.

"I didn't mean anything!" This time his voice was strident. "How can I make you understand that I want us to be friends, if you misconstrue everything I say?"

"How can I not, when every time I talk to you you insult me?" Her tone was as harsh as his.

He hesitated for a moment, and she could hear him taking a deep breath. When he spoke again he sounded anxious but wary. "Kirsten, please, just listen. This is important to me."

She took a deep breath, too, and forced her voice to be reasonably calm. "I'm listening," she assured him.

"When I asked if you had something going with Don, I just meant will you be dating him regularly? If so, I'll respect that and not bother you further, but if not I'd like to take you to dinner and try to straighten out this...hostility between us."

A rush of hope rocked her. She really would like to start seeing him socially. For some reason, she couldn't seem to fight the attraction she felt for him. He was apparently interested in her, too, so maybe it was better to get it out in the open and deal with it. She didn't want any lingering regrets for what might have been once she returned to California.

But first she had to have answers to a couple of questions. "Sam, are you still mad at me for putting dents in your car?"

"No. I was way out of line about that." He sounded a little surprised at the abrupt change of subject. "I'm just glad *you* weren't hurt."

She felt greatly relieved. "Did you get it fixed?"

"Oh yeah, no problem. The body shop billed your insurance and didn't anticipate any difficulty."

That brought a smile to her lips. "Oh, I'm so glad! Does it look all right?"

"Like brand-new!" He really sounded pleased. "You can't even tell it was damaged. I promise you I won't bring the subject up ever again."

Kirsten laughed. "Be careful what you promise. That might be a pretty hard one to keep. You were awfully mad at me."

"I was afraid of you," he said seriously. "That's what fueled my anger."

Kirsten's eyes widened. "Afraid of me? You? But why?"

"It's a bit complicated," he told her. "I can't explain it over the phone. I'm not even sure I can explain it in person, but I'd like to try. There's a restaurant a few miles out of town on the river. If you like, I'll reserve a table on the porch overlooking the water. Barring too many emergencies, I should be able to pick you up about six o'clock. Okay?"

Kirsten couldn't help but laugh. "When you put your mind to it you can be a very persuasive man, Sam Lawford. Six o'clock will be fine."

Coralie was jubilant when Kirsten told her she'd accepted a dinner date with Sam. "The Water's Edge is our one and only upscale restaurant. It has a rustic ambience and the food is delicious. Maybe next time the four of us can go out there together."

"Coralie, stop that!" Kirsten demanded, but she couldn't hide the twinkle in her eyes. "There's not going to be a next time with Sam. He just wants to apologize for his nasty temper."

"Sam doesn't have a nasty temper," Coralie protested. "I don't know how *you* always manage to set him off, but you'll have to admit he's not indifferent to you."

Kirsten pooh-poohed the idea even as she blushed with pleasure.

Sam arrived almost exactly on the stroke of six, and he looked more like a male fashion model than a country doctor in his navy blue suit and maroon paisley tie. Kirsten heard him drive up, and watched from behind the opaque white curtains at the front picture window of Buck's cottage as he got out of his newly refurbished BMW and walked to the house.

He was slender and wore clothes well, and the previous night at the party when the guests resumed swimming after they'd eaten, she'd found out that he looked even better without clothes. Well, at least without anything but skimpy swim briefs that clearly accentuated his masculinity.

Kirsten had been helping Don and her hosts clear away the dirty dishes when she nearly dropped the tray she was carrying after she looked up and saw Sam poised on the diving board. His chest was broad and brawny with a thatch of curly brown hair, and his pectoral muscles rippled when he moved his arms. After he'd executed a perfect jackknife dive she'd kept herself out of sight until he left.

Now he was smiling as he approached the house with an easy gait that was surprisingly graceful for a man.

She waited until he rang the bell, then walked the short distance to let him in. When she opened the door he let his warm gaze roam over her, then murmured, "You look very beautiful."

His voice was husky and his eyes glowed with admiration. She was glad she'd chosen to wear her jade silk sheath with the tank-style top.

She felt the flush of pleasure that she knew was shining from her face. "Thank you," she said unsteadily as she stepped back to let him in. "And you look positively smashing. You wear clothes with such a natural flair."

He looked startled. "Thank you, that's very kind of you."

She shut the door behind him. "Sam, I'm not being kind. I'm being truthful."

This time he grinned. "You're not only beautiful, but you have a strange sense of humor. My so-called flair for clothes consists of wearing slacks, shirt and a tie under a white lab coat in the office and scrubs in surgery."

She looked him up and down in an exaggerated inspection. "I'll bet you look great in scrubs," she taunted, "but I see you're not wearing either of those outfits tonight."

His teasing expression was gone as he gazed into her eyes. "That's because I wanted to make a good impression on you," he murmured seriously, then took her arm and turned her toward the door. "Now, come on. If you're ready let's get out of town before my pesky beeper catches up with me."

The ride through the foothills to the Clearwater River was scenic and relaxing, and the restaurant, situated on the river's edge, was indeed rustic. Built of logs, it looked like a lodge from the outside and inside there was an open room with a massive stone fireplace, red-and-white checked tablecloths on the tables, and thick candles stuck in wine jugs for centerpieces.

Kirsten was impressed, and even more so when the maître d' led them to their table on the wraparound porch overlooking the river and the forested hills on either side.

"If the food here is half as great as the setting I'll consider it one of my all-time favorite places," she said admiringly as she was being seated.

"I'll personally see to it," said the maître d' with a smile as he handed them each a menu. "It would never do to have our newest diner disappointed."

He turned to Sam. "Our cocktail waitress will be right with you, Dr. Sam. Enjoy your evening."

Kirsten grinned. "Another one of your patients, I presume?"

Sam chuckled. "It's a generational thing. My dad delivered him, and I recently delivered his first son."

"I think that's wonderful," she said wistfully. "In the cities today doctors only know their patients by name and medical record, and too many patients don't know their doctors at all except as someone who dispenses medicine and charges what they consider alarmingly high fees."

Their cocktail waitress arrived, a curvy blonde who also called Sam Dr. Sam. He called her Ginger. She wore a very short, tight black skirt and a low-cut ruffled white blouse. Kirsten felt a twinge of distaste although the outfit covered everything it was supposed to, but just barely.

Kirsten waited until Ginger had taken their orders and left before looking at Sam. "Since I assume she's one of your patients, too, I won't ask if all that cleavage is really her."

She'd meant it as a teasing quip, but it came out sounding waspish.

Sam looked at her a moment, then reached over and put his fingers under her chin, turning her face to look at him. "Actually, Ginger isn't one of my patients. She's the wife of the bartender and they've only been here a few months, but do I detect a note of disapproval?" His voice was low, but curious rather than condemning.

Kirsten felt both embarrassed and ashamed. She hadn't been making a moral judgment, but it certainly came out sounding that way. Was it possible she was—? No, it couldn't be. She couldn't be jealous just because the other woman was showing Sam more of her bosom than Kirsten wanted him to see.

"I—I'm sorry," she said, and would have turned away, but he continued to hold her chin so that she had to look at him. "I didn't mean to be catty, truly I didn't."

"I'm sure you didn't," he said and released her.

An uncomfortable silence followed, in which Kirsten couldn't think of anything to say. She was afraid to speak for fear of committing another faux pas.

When Sam didn't speak either, she finally collected her wits and changed the subject. "Coralie told me that your father delivered you and your sisters. Isn't that a bit unusual?"

"Not thirty-odd years ago," he answered. "He was the only doctor in town, and we were all winter births. The road between here and the next physician in Grangeville was too often closed during winter storms to be reliable."

"Do your parents still live here?"

He shook his head. "No. Dad retired a year after I came back home to practice. He and Mom moved to Arizona, where it's warm and sunny all year round."

"So are you still the only doctor in town?"

"No, I have an associate, Michael Taylor, but he and his family are vacationing in Europe this month. That's why I'm so busy. I'm covering two practices." He chuckled. "Plus, of course, the veterinarian's."

They both laughed, and a few minutes later Ginger arrived with their drinks.

Shortly after that the dinner waitress appeared. She was also a friend of Sam's. He introduced Kirsten, and the three of them carried on a light banter while she took their meal orders.

Once she was gone, Kirsten settled back with her strawberry daiquiri and looked around. "This really is a lovely place. I'm sorry they have that magnificent fireplace banked with flowers instead of a fire, though. I love a roaring blaze in a fireplace. It's so...so dreamy."

Sam chuckled and reached out to cover her hand with his. "They do have one during the winter. Stay here long enough and I promise to bring you the first night they light it."

Kirsten sighed. "I wish I could, but don't forget I have to earn a living. They won't hold my job open at the hospital in Eureka once my doctor says I can go back to work."

She sipped her drink and again surveyed the picture-perfect sunset, which streaked across the horizon in shades of burnt orange and shimmering gold. "But we have other things to talk about tonight," she reminded him. "You promised to tell me why you said you were afraid of me the first time we met."

"Ah, yes, so I did," Sam said reluctantly. "I'm afraid I was being indiscreet when I admitted that. I'm not even sure I can explain it to myself, let alone you."

She turned over the hand Sam was covering so that their palms pressed together and their fingers entwined. "Please try," she urged softly.

Sam felt needles prickling all the way up his arm from their joined hands and knew he was powerless to resist her gentle plea.

"I admit I was in a hurry that morning," he began. "As I told you, I'd been called out on an emergency and still had a waiting room full of patients in my office. I wasn't paying as much attention as I should have been, but I did brake for the stop sign. I assumed you would, too, but when I pulled out you went right on through and clobbered me."

She opened her mouth to interrupt, but he hurried on. "I nearly lost control of my car, but I finally got it stopped and hurried over to yours. When I saw you crumpled over your steering wheel with your head in your arms, I was terrified that you'd been badly injured.''

He paused for a moment while he tried to think of how to say what he wanted to without making it sound like a blatant come-on. Finally he just took a deep breath and plunged in.

''Then you sat up and looked at me with those big tawny brown eyes, and I knew I was headed for trouble—''

This time she did break in. ''But I don't understand. Why would I give you trouble? I'd already done all the damage I could do by smashing in the side of your new car.''

''That wasn't even a consideration,'' he assured her. ''At least not at first. It was...'' He shifted uncomfortably. ''It was the warm wave of tenderness I felt for you. Not the concern of a doctor for his patient, but of a man for his woman.''

Kirsten looked startled, and he removed his hand from hers and grabbed his drink. Damn! He sounded like a bad actor mouthing purple prose. Taking a long swallow, he felt the warm buzz of rum fortifying him. ''Look, I don't know how to say this without sounding like I'm hitting on you. I wanted to gather you in my arms and hold you, take you home with me and keep you safe—''

He broke off again, half-afraid she would either slap his face or get up and walk out, but she just sat there looking perplexed.

He fought the urge to pick up her hand again and caress it. ''I know I'm babbling and you think I've lost my mind,'' he said, and his tone was laced with the frustration he felt. ''But nothing like that ever happened to me before, and I sure didn't welcome it. In my confusion I focused on the first thing I saw, which was my wrecked car, and channeled my emotions into the more acceptable feeling of righteous wrath.''

His surprising confession had unleashed a swarm of but-terflies in Kirsten's stomach that made her feel buoyant with happiness even as she struggled to understand. "But why would you rather be mad at me than have tender feelings for me?"

"It's a long story, and I'm not even sure myself," he admitted. "For one thing, I'm a confirmed bachelor. I have my reasons and they have nothing to do with you, but marriage simply isn't in my foreseeable future, so I shy away from romantic entanglements."

She nodded. This was exactly what Coralie had told her. "But you do date...?"

He grinned. "Sure I do. You should know. Haven't I been pestering you all week to go out with me?"

She smiled, but his expression sobered as he continued. "I enjoy the occasional company of women the same as any other man does, but I don't want any deep emotional involvements. That's why I was so chagrined when we first met. I didn't like the feelings you aroused in me, because they were off-limits and I couldn't control them."

The man wasn't making sense. "But people can't control their feelings," she said firmly. "You can control your actions, but your emotions are involuntary. All you can do is deal with them."

"No!" he said harshly. "Emotions can be controlled. I've been doing it for years, but in your case the accident happened so unexpectedly and so fast that I didn't have time to prepare...to put up a guard...."

His whole demeanor mirrored his determination. He was absolutely certain he was right, and it was evident that she could only lose this argument. He wasn't about to admit that he was at the mercy of his passions the same as everyone else.

Her disappointment was painful, but she decided to approach the subject from another angle. "So you were wrong about your romantic protectiveness toward me? It was just a trick of the mind and you got over it?"

"No," he murmured in answer to her questioning observation. "It wasn't a trick and I didn't get over it, but I found a way to make it nonthreatening."

Sam reached out to her and his finger caressed her cheek so gently that it was like a feather touch, but a touch that sent tiny shivers all through her. "And...and how was that?" She had to concentrate hard to keep her mind on what they were talking about.

Much to her dismay he removed his finger from her cheek, but in the next instant he picked up her hand and engulfed it in his own on the table.

"I've always tried to be an honorable man, Kirsten," he said in a tone that was more businesslike than romantic. "I don't get involved with a woman until I'm sure she understands that nothing permanent can ever come of it. That's why I'm telling you all this. I'm very attracted to you, and I want to see you while you're here, but I don't want you to get hurt. Our relationship won't go any deeper than you want it to."

He made a self-deprecating grimace. "Hell, I'm really botching this, aren't I? I guess, to put it bluntly, what I'm trying to say is I can let down my guard with you because you're safe. You'll be leaving in two weeks to take up your life in California, and we'll probably never see each other again."

Kirsten pondered his remarks. They sounded like her own arguments to Coralie. Mainly that she wasn't looking for a husband, and she had no desire to become involved in a month-long vacation romance. Those were altogether too risky. She could lose her heart as well as her peace of mind.

Now, much against her better judgment, she was fast changing her mind about Sam, and he was so obviously agonizing over his effort to explain his feelings without offending her that she couldn't help but feel for him.

And the last thing she wanted to do was discourage him. It seemed as if he was really serious about wanting to spend time with her, but he was equally adamant about not extending their potential...friendship, liaison, *whatever*...past the two-week limit.

"How can you be so sure that if we're, uh, close during the time I'm here, you won't miss me when I'm gone?"

He looked at her sadly. "I will miss you." His voice was gravelly. "How could I not? But you'll be out of sight and reach, and I'll be busy. I don't have much time for daydreaming even if I wanted to, and since I don't want to I'll just concentrate on something else."

That hurt, and she withdrew her hand from his. "Well, thanks a lot." Her tone was sarcastic. "It's nice to be needed."

His expression changed to one of contrition. "I'm sorry. I was afraid you wouldn't understand. Needing a woman is exactly what I want to avoid. I let that happen once, to my everlasting regret. I don't intend to repeat that mistake."

Kirsten's heart sank. Belinda! He was referring to his ex-fiancée, Belinda Evans. So Coralie was right, he hadn't gotten over her!

"I know," she muttered before she could stop herself.

He sat up straight. "What do you know?"

Oh darn, now she was in for it, and it wouldn't do any good to try to deny she knew what he was asking. She ducked her head so she wouldn't have to look at him. "I know that you had an unhappy love affair with a woman who married another man," she said in a tiny voice.

He put his fingers under her chin and lifted her face. "Did Jim Buckley tell you that?" He looked both angry and disappointed.

"No!" She couldn't let Sam think Jim had been gossiping about him. Their friendship was too deep and important to let a misunderstanding come between them.

"Truly, Sam," she insisted. "Jim didn't say a thing. It was Coralie, but she only mentioned it because she was trying to explain to me why you were behaving like such a jerk."

Oh, God, couldn't she say anything without garbling it? "Oh, I mean... That is...." It took her a few seconds to see that he was grinning.

He released her chin. "A jerk, huh," he drawled. "As I remember, you called me a bastard. Do I get a choice, or did you two lovely ladies mean I was both?"

Kirsten was so relieved that he was taking it well that she decided to play along. "Both," she answered promptly, "but we've forgiven you."

Before Sam could answer the waitress brought their dinner.

The food was delicious. Hearty and plentiful, with more calories than Kirsten usually allowed herself for a whole day. She appeased her conscience by remembering that she'd lost weight during her recent illness so she could afford to pig out now.

By the time they finished eating it was dark, and the candles in the wine jugs on each table had been lit, casting a soft glow. It was light enough to eat by, but dark enough for privacy.

After the waitress took away their empty dessert dishes and poured them more coffee, Sam again reached for Kirsten's hand. They were seated intimately close at a small, round table, and her heart pounded when she felt his leg press gently against her own.

Her good sense warned her to move away, but she couldn't bring herself to do that. If this was just going to be a short-term relationship, she might as well enjoy it while it lasted. As her mom always said, "nothing ventured, nothing gained."

The problem was, her mom didn't have this particular venture in mind, and Kirsten suspected she might gain much more than she wanted to. Such as an unplanned pregnancy, if their emotions got out of control, and almost certainly a broken heart.

RIV'LED HEARTSTONE

Chapter Six

Kirsten was fully enjoying the quiet intimacy of candlelight and conversation over the peaceful sound of water rippling down the rocky bed of the river when it was shattered by the high-pitched beep-beep of Sam's pager.

He muttered an oath and reached in his pocket for it. "I'm sorry," he said as he pushed his chair back and stood. "I have to make a phone call."

He hurried off only to return a few minutes later looking grim. "There's been a two-car accident and the injured have been taken to the hospital. Since I'm the only doctor available—"

"Of course," Kirsten interrupted as she stood. "We have to leave immediately."

Within a short while they were in the car and heading toward Copper Canyon on the two-lane highway. "I'm really sorry, Kirsten," Sam said, his tone brusque with frustration. "I'd hoped we could spend the whole evening together, but now I won't even have time to take you out to the farm. I hope you don't mind coming with me to the hospital. We can call Jim from there and ask him to come in and pick you up. I'm sure he won't mind.''

She was disappointed, too, but it certainly wasn't Sam's fault. She put her hand on his arm. ''Sam, I'm a nurse, remember? I know all about doctors' interrupted social lives. I'd hoped we could spend the rest of the evening together, too, but that's the risk we gals take when we date a physician. I understand. Please don't apologize.''

He reached over and briefly covered her hand with his own. ''I'm beginning to understand why I was so attracted to you the very first time I saw you,'' he murmured softly, then returned his attention to his driving.

The warmth in his tone washed over her like a soothing panacea, but she was at a loss for a way to respond. Instead, she changed the subject. ''Do you know what happened and how serious the injuries are?'' she asked.

''It was a head-on collision involving two cars filled with teenagers playing road games.'' His voice was filled with disgust. ''Thank God no one was killed, but when are kids going to learn that they're not immortal? There were nine of them in those two cars, and all have fairly serious injuries. There are apparent broken bones, but we won't know the full degree of damage until we do X rays and tests.''

The picture his words brought to Kirsten's mind was horrifying. ''How awful,'' she said with a shudder. ''Can you handle all those patients by yourself?''

He shrugged. ''It depends on how serious their injuries are. We may have to call on the two physicians in Grangeville for help. We're also short of qualified nurses. There are only two RNs on our staff, and neither of them has had training in trauma cases. The rest of the nursing personnel are medical assistants.''

''But I'm a registered nurse,'' Kirsten blurted, ''and I've had emergency-room experience. I'd be glad to help out if you need me. I'd really love to get back to work again, even if for only a few hours.''

He looked at her and frowned. "Are you sure you're up to it? You're still on medical leave—"

"I'm fine," she assured him, "and it would only be for a few hours."

He reached down and took her hand. "In that case I'd welcome your assistance."

A short time later Sam zoomed into his parking space at the back of the hospital and brought his car to a screeching halt. They both got out and rushed through the wide double doors into the emergency area.

It was the smallest ER Kirsten had ever seen, consisting of a large, open space with a partition three-quarters of the way down the middle. To the right of the partition and straight ahead of them was a registration desk with benches attached to the walls around it. There were a few chairs, and the space was filled with people both sitting and milling around. She assumed they were the parents and relatives of the wounded kids.

To the left were three examining cubicles, and in the narrow hallway between them and the partition stood several gurneys holding injured adolescents. Various medical personnel moved rapidly through the restricted space as they hurried from one patient to another.

There was a lot of sobbing, wailing and raised voices on both sides, which lifted the noise level to a continuous roar.

Sam took one look at the crowd in the waiting room and put his arm around Kirsten's waist as he rushed her to the left side of the partition. "Come on," he muttered, "I want to get out of here before somebody recognizes me. There's no time to be slowed down and badgered with questions that I don't have answers to."

Once they were inside the partition, he caught up with one of the scurrying nurses. "Myra, this is Kirsten. She's an RN and has volunteered to help. Please see that she's properly garbed and show her where she can wash up and change."

* * *

Four hours later Kirsten sank wearily against the wall in the now empty hallway and wiped the back of her arm across her sweaty brow. She was exhausted. They'd treated all nine teenagers for injuries that ranged from one deep laceration to multiple fractures. The hospital had managed to recruit one physician and another nurse from Grangeville to help in the emergency, which was a godsend, but even so they'd all been working at top speed without a break.

Fortunately there didn't seem to be any internal injuries, although one of the boys, who had broken ribs, was being admitted overnight for observation. Two other kids had been admitted into the hospital as well. The girl with multiple fractures and a boy with a head wound, who was still unconscious.

Now the emergency room was empty except for the regular staff on duty, and they were still washing up—something Kirsten intended to do just as soon as she could convince her shaking knees and aching feet to walk to the nurses' lounge in the regular part of the hospital.

She finally found the energy to push herself away from the wall and start up the hall when she heard the automatic doors open behind her and a voice call, "Nurse, wait. I want to know how my brother is."

The voice sounded familiar and she turned to confront Richard McBride. He was wearing his blue uniform pants and shirt, and he looked surprised. "Kirsten, what are you doing here? And dressed like that?" She knew he was referring to the scrubs the hospital had supplied and the stretch slippers somebody had loaned her.

"Hello, Richard," she said wearily. "Don't you remember? I'm a nurse. I was with Sam at a restaurant when he got the call about the accident, so I volunteered to help. What's this about your brother? Was he in the crash?"

Richard looked anxious. "Yeah. His name's Barry... Barry McBride. He's sixteen and has a head injury. I've been keeping in touch by phone, but I couldn't get away from the site of the investigation until now.''

He was moving about restlessly. ''Is he going to be all right? Are my mom and dad still here?''

''I'm sorry, but you'll have to talk to the doctor,'' Kirsten said. ''I didn't know any of the people who were in and out of here, and we were so busy that I didn't always catch the names of the patients. I do know that we had three head injuries, but—''

She heard footsteps coming from the opposite direction and looked back to see Sam coming toward them, still wearing his white lab coat. ''Oh, here comes Sam now.''

He hurried his pace and stopped beside them. ''Rick, I'm glad to see you.'' His tone was brisk. ''I'm almost certain that Barry's going to be all right. He has a concussion and is still unconscious. There's a little swelling, but we can't detect any sign of cerebral bleeding. I've got him in intensive care, which is usual procedure until he regains consciousness, but your parents are sure he's at death's door.''

Richard nodded. ''Yeah, I'm not surprised. You know how Mom and Dad are about Barry. He was their late-in-life baby, and they can't accept the fact that he's almost a grown man.'' He grimaced. ''Not that that's hard to understand after this dangerous stunt. If I'd known he was going to play chicken with his car, I'd have seen to it that he never got a license.''

Sam frowned. ''Was he driving one of the cars?''

Richard hesitated. ''None of those kids are very forthcoming with information, but it looks like he might have been. One of the cars was his, the one Mom and Dad bought him for his sixteenth birthday. Can I see him?''

Sam nodded. ''Sure. You know the way, but do me a favor, will you? Try to get your folks to go home. They can't do anything sitting around here stewing, and I'm more worried about Dorothy than I am about Barry. She's still recovering from that open-heart surgery she had a few months ago, and all this stress isn't going to do her any good."

"I'll do my best," Richard assured him, "but once Mom makes up her mind about something I've never had much luck trying to get her to change it."

He left and Sam looked at Kirsten, then put his arm around her and encouraged her to lean against him. "You look like you're about wiped out," he observed anxiously. "I should have paid more attention and not let you work so hard."

"Don't be silly," she said as she wilted against his chest, grateful for the support. "I'm not your responsibility. I admit I'm tired, but I'm okay. Besides, you needed the help."

"That I did," he agreed, "and you were superb. I don't know how I can ever thank you, but I will see to it that the hospital pays you for your time and expertise."

She raised her head to look at him. "No, Sam, please don't do that. I volunteered my services, and I don't want to be paid. For one thing I'm not licensed to work in Idaho."

He opened his mouth to say something, but she hurried on. "I know, we could get around that since this was a onetime emergency situation, but I have to tell you, Doctor, that working with you was an experience I won't soon forget. You're an excellent physician, and I'm in a position to know. I've worked with a lot of them, and you rank right up there at the top in my estimation. It was a privilege to assist you."

Sam put both arms around her and hugged her. "Thank you," he murmured as she once more buried her face in his chest. "Your approval is important to me. I hope I can live up to it."

For a moment they just stood there quietly as he held her, but then the double doors opened and closed again as someone came in, and he released her with a wry grin.

"It's probably not good public relations for the only doctor in town to stand around in the ER hallway making out with a nurse,'' he teased, ''so let's change our clothes and get the hell out of here.''

Fifteen minutes later they were in Sam's car driving toward the Buckley farm. Kirsten relaxed against the back of the seat, exhausted but happy. She'd meant it when she told him that working with him had been a great experience for her. As they ministered to their patients side by side, it hadn't taken long for her to realize that he was a caring and dedicated physician. Why wasn't he on the staff of a big-city hospital making loads of money, having weekends off and becoming well-known for his exceptional skills?

The only way she could find out was to ask him. ''Sam, I know your dad practiced here for many years, but why did you come back to a small town like Copper Canyon and take over his practice, when you're good enough to establish an extremely successful and well-paying one in any big city?''

He reached over to take her hand and held it between them. ''Thank you for the vote of confidence, honey, but I didn't study medicine to get rich and famous. I'm doing exactly what I set out to do. It had always been my father's dream...and mine,'' he hastened to add, ''that I'd work with him until he retired and then take over. There's a far greater need for physicians in rural areas than in urban ones, and filling that need is what practicing medicine means to me.''

Kirsten squeezed his hand. He really was a nice man. ''That's very noble of you,'' she said softly.

''Noble!'' he growled, and withdrew his hand from hers to put it back on the steering wheel. ''There's nothing noble about it. It's the essence of the Hippocratic oath I took. The whole idea of becoming a physician is to save *lives*, not make money. Some of the patients I've treated since I've been in practice here would have died if there hadn't been medical care available, and knowing I was here for them means more to me than any high fee I could have collected in a city that is oversupplied with doctors.''

Oh, damn! Now she'd done it again. Why couldn't she seem to talk to Sam for more than a few minutes without antagonizing him? She'd only wanted to tell him how much she admired him, and instead it came out sounding like she was putting him down.

Before she could get her thoughts collected and say anything, he braked suddenly and turned into the driveway of the Buckley farm. As he did so he flung one arm across her to keep her from getting tossed around.

''I'm sorry,'' he said as he approached the large darkened farmhouse. ''I wasn't paying attention and almost missed the turn. Are you all right?''

She was shaken up, but her seat belt had held her firmly in place. ''I'm okay,'' she assured him. ''I'm sorry if I distracted you.''

By this time Sam had steered the car across the barnyard and parked in front of the cottage. He shut off the engine and reached out to her.

''Come here, Kirsten,'' he said softly, and without hesitation she unfastened her seat belt and snuggled into his arms.

The bucket seats limited their contact to above the waist, but she put her head on his shoulder and he rubbed his cheek in her hair. ''You've been distracting me ever since we met,'' he murmured, ''but I'm the one who's sorry. I shouldn't have bristled at you like that. You were only being sweet and complimentary.''

He stretched out and pulled her closer. ''You couldn't have known that the scarcity of physicians in rural areas is a touchy subject with me. It seems that so few of us want to bury ourselves in the boondocks where we are desperately needed, and instead vie with one another for the prestigious positions in big-city medical centers.''

She put her arms around his neck and stroked his nape.

How could she fault him when he apologized so lovingly? "I understand what you're saying," she said against the side of his throat, "but at the risk of getting bawled out again I have to tell you that in my book you're a bona fide hero, whether you like it or not."

"I love it," he admitted, "and I promise to never 'bawl you out' again. Am I forgiven?"

"There's nothing to forgive," she assured him. "Don't you know that heroes never make mistakes?"

He brushed the hair back from her face and kissed her temple. "This one is about to," he said huskily, "because I've reached the end of my endurance and unless you stop me I'm going to kiss you good-night."

Her heart thudded, and her nerve ends tingled with expectation. "Don't count on me to stop you," she whispered in his ear. "I intend to be an eager participant."

"Oh, Kirsten," he moaned. "Do you know what you're doing to me?" He put his hand under her jaw and raised her head so that her face was directly beneath his.

He brushed his mouth across hers, then back again before she could respond. It was almost too gentle to be a kiss, but it made her feel light and buoyant, like floating on a cloud of soft, white down feathers.

She clutched a fistful of his hair to keep herself earthbound, then asked seductively, "Could you do that again?"

His brown eyes darkened as he kissed first one side of her mouth, then the other, before covering it with his own. Her lips parted and so did his, but instead of deepening the kiss he caught her lower lip and sucked gently on it, sending tiny shivers down her spine.

His hands stroked her back and shoulders, but he painstakingly avoided more erotic caresses. She could feel his heart pounding and his labored breathing.

His obviously hard-won control was a powerful turn-on. Most of the men she'd dated were all over her the minute they got her alone. She hated that, and she appreciated

Sam's restraint. It made her feel cherished and respected, although she wasn't sure she could have resisted him if he'd wanted to be more physical. Her control was as hard-won as his.

"Much as I hate to break this up, I think it's in the best interest of both of us if we do," he murmured as he closed each of her eyelids with a gentle kiss. "I'll walk you to your door."

He kissed her once more quickly on the mouth, then opened his door and got out of the car. Kirsten also got out, and Sam took her arm as they strolled up the lighted walkway.

She rummaged in her purse for her key and gave it to him. He opened the screen and unlocked the door, then returned the key. "I apologize again for our interrupted evening," he said, and ran the back of his fingers down her cheek, "but thank you for being so sweet and understanding. And also for working with me in the emergency. I don't know if you noticed, but I always called for you when I needed an assistant."

She understood now why a cat purred with contentment when it was stroked. "I didn't notice," she admitted softly, "but that's because I was so busy making sure I was first in line when you needed help."

He looked pleased. "We make a good team, don't we?"

"Yes, we do," she admitted, but she knew they could never work together. Not without becoming lovers, and that wouldn't be enough for Kirsten. If she ever became intimate with Sam she would want all of him. His past, present and future, all tied up in a lifetime package.

But he'd warned her that would never happen. He'd been very up-front and open about it, and she knew he was adamant. If she got involved with him, she would have no one but herself to blame when it ended in heartbreak.

"I want you to promise me that you'll go right to bed

and sleep as long as you can," Sam admonished. "And call me immediately if you have any signs of asthma."

"Yes, Doctor," she said impishly. "Whatever you say."

He smiled and cupped her head with his hands, then tilted her chin upward. "Don't tempt me," he pleaded. "I don't think you're fully aware of just how strongly I'd like to have you do my bidding."

Slowly he lowered his face and took her mouth. Again her lips parted, and this time he rimmed them with the tip of his tongue. He tasted of fruity wine and chocolate mousse, but before she could explore further he raised his head, murmured "good night" and bounded back down the steps.

The digital clock on Sam's dashboard told him it was 12:43 a.m. as he sped back toward town. No wonder Kirsten was so exhausted. She'd been on her feet at the tail end of the day for four hours straight. Ordinarily that wouldn't be too great a hardship for a nurse—they were used to it—but she was still getting over a serious illness and hadn't worked or even been especially active for more than two months.

No matter how she tried to make light of it, he could see in hindsight that he should have insisted she take frequent rest breaks. Instead, he'd selfishly kept her at his side for the whole time.

Sure, he'd been swamped with patients and responsibility, and she was an excellent assistant, but that was no excuse. Her good health was more important to him than anything else right now, and he should have kept that in mind instead of pouring duties on her every chance he got.

He'd found out quickly that he could rely on her to carry out his orders, and to use her own good judgment in procedure on injuries she was qualified to treat. She'd not only carried out his directives almost before he'd ordered them, but she was good at delegating duties to those who worked under her. She kept things running smoothly so he could give all his attention to his patients, but in doing so she might have risked another attack of asthma or a relapse of the virus that had made her so sick.

The lights of the small town loomed ahead of him, and suddenly he realized just how tired he was. And not only because of the stress and strain tonight. It was a cumulative tiredness that had been building up for the past three weeks. Ever since his associate had gone off on vacation with his family and left Sam with double duty.

They each had more patients than they could comfortably accommodate, and when one doctor was out of commission for any reason the other one was swamped. Sam hadn't had a day off since Mike had left. He even held office hours on Saturday and Sunday mornings just to keep up.

That must be why he was so vulnerable to Kirsten. His bone-weary exhaustion had lowered his resistance and left him needy. Not so much for sex, although there was that, too, but for the soft, loving embrace of a woman. Any woman.

That thought brought him up short and he frowned. No, not just any woman. Even as a high-school, college and medical student he'd never been the type to fall into bed with just any willing partner.

Of course during those years he'd spent most of his leisure time with Belinda. Immediately, the familiar pain of loss and loneliness overcame him. Damn! How had Belinda managed to creep into his musings? Over the years he'd learned to hold her at bay pretty successfully.

He'd discovered early on that if he dwelled on her betrayal he wasn't good for anything, and with some counseling he'd made the effort to pull himself together and look forward instead of back. He'd been twenty-seven years old when Belinda walked out on him, after they'd been inseparable since kindergarten. That was when he first understood the agonizing truth of the cliché, "painful as being torn in half."

That was exactly how he had felt, as though half of him had been torn away leaving the other half broken and bleeding.

He shuddered, and turned off the highway and headed north toward his house.

He was never going through pain like that again. Nothing was worth it. Not even love. Especially not love, and he would damn well remember that. He might be despondent and lonely now and then in his self-imposed bachelor state, but nothing could be as bad as the agony Belinda had put him through. Absolutely nothing!

The shadowed outline of his house jolted him back to the present, and he drove into his driveway and pushed the remote-control button that opened the garage door. When he was inside he turned off the engine, then pushed the button again to close the door and sat in the dark brooding.

It was becoming more and more obvious by the moment that he could never have a superficial romance with Kirsten Reinhold. He wasn't sure what it was about her that attracted him so, but he meant to put a stop to it before things got out of control.

He should have let well enough alone right from the beginning and stayed away from her once they got the problem of the damage to his car settled. But no, he had to play with fire and pursue her.

He'd known that the feelings she aroused in him were dangerous, but instead of facing that fact and beating a hasty retreat he'd denied it. He'd told himself she was a sexy lady and he was single and available. If they lit sparks off one another, fine. If not, there was no harm done.

No harm? Hah! He'd vastly overestimated his ability to casually light a fuse without setting off a bomb.

He took the keys out of the ignition and opened the door, flooding the inside of the car with light. He'd intended to ask Kirsten to go to a movie tomorrow night, even started to mention it once, but something interrupted them. At least that saved him from one more mistake. He wouldn't be asking her for any more dates. In fact, if he could prevent it he wouldn't be seeing or speaking to her again while she was visiting the Buckleys.

Of course, he still needed to call her in the morning to make sure she wasn't suffering any aftereffects from working so hard this evening. After all, he was the only doctor in town. It was his duty to make sure she was all right.

Kirsten slept in until ten o'clock and woke feeling rested and energized, with the imprint of Sam's tender kisses still thrilling her.

Thrilling? Wasn't she a little old to be *thrilled* by a man's kiss? Apparently not, because that was the only word she could think of to describe her reaction to Sam's caresses. Thrilled and excited. Like a teenager with her first crush.

But what she felt for him was no crush. On the other hand it couldn't be love, either. Could it? She'd only known him for two weeks, and most of that time they'd spent sparring with each other. That was no way to fall in love.

Still, what did she know? She'd never been in love before. Maybe she should talk it over with Coralie. If any couple was ever in love, it was Coralie and Jim. The magnetism positively radiated between them.

Kirsten got out of bed, showered and pulled on jeans and a T-shirt. Her mind made up, she headed over to the big house for her morning coffee and to help Coralie fix dinner while they chatted.

Coralie was cutting up chickens when Kirsten arrived, and the air was redolent with the aroma of something chocolate baking in the oven.

"Oh God, Coralie, this kitchen always smells so good," she said rapturously. "Do you know I've already put on three pounds since I've been here? I'll be positively chubby by the time I get home again.''

Coralie eyed her critically and hooted. "That I'll have to see. You lost at least ten pounds while you were sick. I'm delighted to know you're putting some of them back on. Pour yourself a cup of coffee, and I'll heat up a couple of muffins for you. You haven't had breakfast yet, have you?''

"Thanks a bunch," Kirsten groaned good-naturedly as she headed for the coffeepot. "I'm gonna make you help pay for the new wardrobe I'll need if I stay here much longer. You know I can't resist your cooking."

Coralie grinned. "So quit your complainin' and tell me all about your date with Sam last night."

Kirsten's eyebrows rose dramatically. "*All* about it?"

"Every second of it," Coralie teased, "but first how about cutting to the action. Did he kiss you good-night?"

Kirsten stifled a laugh as she sat down at the table with her cup of coffee. "You always were the one who read the last chapter of a mystery novel first, but this time you're going to get the story in sequence, so stop dithering and listen."

She told Coralie all about her evening with Sam, even repeating what he'd told her about his intention to remain an uncommitted bachelor for life. But when she got to the part about the accident, Coralie stopped her.

"I haven't heard about that," she said, shocked. "Was anyone killed? Or seriously injured? Why didn't you call me? I'm a nurse, too. I'd have been glad to help."

"There were no fatalities," Kirsten assured her, "and although there were numerous lacerations, contusions and broken bones, only three of the kids were kept at the hospital. I didn't call you because they recruited a doctor and RN from Grangeville. Now shut up and let me finish. I'm just about to come to the X-rated part."

Coralie's eyes flashed with amusement. "By all means, continue."

Kirsten told her friend about Sam's good-night kisses, but without going into detail. That was private. A lovely moment of lovemaking to be hugged tightly and shared only with him.

Coralie understood, as Kirsten had known she would, and respected Kirsten's privacy by switching to a different view of the subject.

"So when are you seeing him again?" she asked excitedly.

"Oh, well, I..." Kirsten floundered, then tried again. "That is, we...we..." She made a hopeless gesture with her hands. "Come to think of it, we didn't make another date. I guess we were both too exhausted to bring the subject up."

"He'll no doubt call you," Coralie said, "but he knows he'll see you Sunday."

Kirsten blinked. "He does? How come? What's going on Sunday?"

Now it was Coralie's turn to blink. "Did I forget to tell you? Oh, damn, I'm sorry. Sunday is Jim's birthday, and he and Sam always get together on their birthdays. Sam and several other close friends are coming over for supper. We'll barbecue steaks and have potatoes and corn on the cob roasted in the coals. That's Jim's favorite meal. And of course there'll be ice cream and birthday cake with thirty-six candles on it."

"Sounds wonderful," Kirsten said. "Sam didn't say anything about it. Are you sure you didn't forget to tell him, too?"

Coralie looked thoughtful. "Hmm. I thought Jim was going to talk to him about it, but maybe I got my signals crossed. Remind me to ask Jim when he comes in at noon."

A couple of hours later they were just finishing up the midday meal when the phone rang. "I'll get it," Jim said as he pushed back his chair. "I'm expecting a call from the bank."

There was a phone in the kitchen, but Jim chose to take it upstairs where it was quieter and no doubt more private. He'd been gone only a few minutes when they heard his footsteps bounding down the stairs.

"It's for you, Kirsten," he said. "Sam. You can take it in our bedroom upstairs if you'd like."

Kirsten jumped up and headed out of the kitchen. "Remind him about Sunday," Coralie called after her.

The telephone was on the desk in the corner of the large master bedroom that Jim used as an office. She was slightly breathless when she picked it up. "Sam? This is Kirsten." Her tone sounded seductive, although she hadn't meant it to.

At the other end of the line Sam hesitated. Her sexy tone of voice erased everything from his mind but his urgent desire to see her, touch her, hold her again in his arms and kiss that sweet, ripe mouth.

"Y-yes, Kirsten," he stammered, then paused again to take a deep breath and get a grip on his emotions. "I'm calling to ask if you're all right. I would have gotten in touch sooner, but this is the first break I've had all morning. Did you sleep well? Is your breathing okay?"

He couldn't keep the anxiety out of his voice, but he hoped it sounded like the kind a doctor would have for his patient, instead of the type a lover would experience.

Apparently it didn't, because she wasn't at all put off. "I'm just fine," she said happily. "I slept for almost ten hours straight and woke up feeling rested and full of energy. How about you? Did you get enough rest?"

No, he hadn't, as a matter of fact. He'd spent hours trying to forget those soft, chaste kisses she'd so willingly shared with him. At the time he hadn't known they were addictive.

"I slept okay," he hedged. "I only had one call and that

was from the hospital. I'd asked them to let me know when Barry McBride regained consciousness."

"Is he going to be all right?" She sounded truly concerned, as if Barry were a friend instead of just another patient.

"Yeah, he'll have a humongous headache for a while, but he's alert and functioning."

"Oh, I'm so glad," she said with an audible sigh of relief. "Richard was really worried...."

A sharp jab of jealousy jolted Sam, and it appalled him even more than it hurt. So that was the cause of her concern. Her personal interest was in Richard.

Well, so what. Sam knew he had no right to be jealous of her interest in Rick McBride. If he wasn't going to court Kirsten, it was none of his business if she was attracted to someone else.

You can't have it both ways, fella. Either ask her out again or cut this conversation off right now and forget about her.

Oh yeah, sure, forget about her. And just how was he supposed to do that when he ached with wanting her?

Chapter Seven

Kirsten's raised voice cut through Sam's musing and brought his attention back to the telephone in his hand.

"Sam, are you still there?"

"Umm... Oh... Oh, yes," he stuttered. "Yes, I'm still here, but I've got to cut this short. I have patients waiting—"

"I'm sure you have," she said quickly, "but can I just have one more minute of your time? Coralie asked me to remind you that Sunday is Jim's birthday and you're invited over for supper."

Sam blinked. "What? Oh, that's right..."

Damn! He'd been so busy that he'd forgotten Jim's birthday was coming up in a few days. Now what was he going to do? No excuse short of being in a coma would be acceptable for declining that invitation. His and Jim's birthdays were only two weeks apart and each was always included in the other's celebration. Had been since they were toddlers.

But he couldn't show up Sunday. Kirsten would be there, and he'd just vowed to himself not to see her again!

"Sam! Is something the matter? Answer me!" Kirsten sounded a little frantic, and he realized that she was waiting for him to finish his comment.

"I'm sorry," he said as he tried to marshal his thoughts and come up with a good reason for avoiding the party. "I should have let Coralie know sooner, but I'm...I'm tied up that day."

Oh hell, there was no way they would accept that flimsy excuse. "I mean, I...I have office hours on Sunday mornings while my associate's on vacation."

"That won't be a problem," Kirsten assured him. "It's a barbecue and it starts at five o'clock in the evening."

Sam was sweating, and it wasn't because of the heat outside. He never had learned to lie, and he was really botching the attempt now.

There was nothing he could do but tell her he would be there, and use the time between now and then to think up a good reason for not going after all.

He swallowed and spoke into the phone. "Good. Then of course I'll come, but right now I really do have to get back to my patients. I'll see you Sunday. Bye."

He dropped the instrument into its cradle and slumped down in his chair.

The Buckley family and Kirsten spent most of their spare time sprucing up the large flower garden at the back of the big house in preparation for the party. They didn't have a swimming pool, but there was a built-in barbecue and enough space for setting up tables and chairs around the blazing red, peach and yellow rosebushes, and the beds of zinnias, chrysanthemums, marigolds and asters in brilliant shades of gold, pink and violet.

By Saturday night all the food that could be fixed ahead of time was prepared and stored in the refrigerator and the garden was a riot of blossoms and color. It wasn't going to be a big party. They'd invited several of Jim's closest friends, and each of his daughters had been allowed to ask a guest of her own age. Most of them would be strangers to Kirsten, but that didn't matter. As long as Sam would be there she didn't need anybody else to keep her company.

Sam's temporary office hours ran longer than usual on Sunday, and by the time he'd seen his last patient, grabbed a sandwich and coffee at Kathy's Kitchen on Main Street, and finally made it home it was after two o'clock. Much too late to back out of Jim's party now!

Ever since talking to Kirsten, he'd told himself that as soon as he had a few minutes to spare he would think up a good pretense to avoid the party, but he'd kept putting it off. No time, interruptions, and he'd been unable to come up with a plausible reason. The excuses for malingering mounted, until now the only possible way to get out of the party would be to plead illness, and Jim knew better than anybody else that Sam was never sick. In fact he was a model of excellent health, and he'd been seeing patients all morning, so that deception was out of the question.

Much as he hated to face the truth, he had to admit that he hadn't really wanted to stay away from the birthday celebration, *or from Kirsten.* So okay, he was breaking his own rules, but damn it, he wanted to be with her. He loved the musical sound of her voice, her happy laughter and the sexy way her lips quivered when he kissed her.

That thought made him break out in a sweat, and he uttered an oath. What was the matter with him anyway? He'd kissed lots of women in his almost thirty-six years, so why was this one special?

He'd learned his lesson from Belinda well. In the eight years since she'd left, he'd managed to avoid becoming emotionally entangled with any of the ladies he'd kissed, and he could do the same with Kirsten. It was just a matter of mind over temptation.

The phrase *famous last words* rang in his head, but he ignored it.

There were two guest cars already parked on the spacious grounds of the Buckley farm when Sam brought his Beemer to a stop beside them. He was wearing plum-colored shorts and a matching pullover shirt, and his stomach muscles were tied in knots. His heart raced as he scooped the hastily purchased and wrapped gift from the passenger seat and opened the car door.

Good Lord, you would think he'd never looked forward to seeing a pretty woman before, and this wasn't even a date. Just a birthday party to which they'd both been invited.

He'd started around the car when he saw Kirsten coming toward him from the rose garden looking absolutely irresistible in white short shorts and a white peasant blouse with a low, ruffled neckline. Her long, slender legs were tanned, and her curvy hips undulated with a natural rhythm that made him long to put his hands on either side of them, pull her close and swing and sway with her. There was a big smile on her face and a sparkle in her warm brown eyes.

His control shattered, and he put the package down on the trunk of the auto and held out his arms. She ran into them and they closed tightly around her without any prompting from him. He couldn't help it. These past few days had been lonely and barren without her, and he needed her heat and her loving embrace.

Before he could capture her mouth with his, he saw Jim and Coralie several feet behind her. Disappointed, he kissed her forehead instead and murmured, "God, but it's good to see you."

Jim and Coralie were both beaming when they reached Sam and Kirsten. Sam released her and the two men grabbed each other in a boxers' hug. "So how's the birthday boy?'' Sam asked playfully as he threw a simulated punch and handed Jim the gift. "Here, this is for you. Damn, but you don't look a day over forty."

Jim choked on a laugh and whacked Sam on the back. "That's because I'm only thirty-six, you young whippersnapper, but just wait. You've got a birthday comin' up in only two more weeks. I'll getcha then, Son."

"I'm sure you will, Dad," Sam teased back, then reached for a laughing Coralie and kissed her on the cheek before taking Kirsten's hand as the two couples hurried back to join the others in the garden.

For the first hour the women visited while the men drank beer and explored the farm and its animals, machinery and crops. Gloria and Amber entertained their guests, both girls, with recordings by their favorite rock groups in their bedrooms upstairs.

By six o'clock the aroma of charred mahogany and grilling steaks smothered in homemade barbecue sauce drove everyone back to the brick grill and the buffet table. Sam latched on to Kirsten for his supper partner, and they shared a table with Dave and Sally Roberts, the owners and publishers of the *Star Journal*, Copper Canyon's weekly newspaper. They were a couple in their mid-thirties whom Kirsten hadn't met before, but they were obviously good friends of both Jim and Sam.

"You'll be coming to the potluck supper and dance next Saturday, won't you?" Sally asked Kirsten.

Kirsten wrinkled her brow and tried to remember if Coralie had mentioned plans to attend such an event. "I...I don't remember hearing anything about it," she admitted.

"Oh, it's a monthly event. It's sponsored by the Masonic Lodge at their hall. Everyone brings a casserole, salad or dessert to share, and we have live music when we can get it, otherwise it's recordings. Practically everyone in town turns out for it. If you don't have a date, I'll be happy to fix you up with—''

"She has a date," Sam interrupted, as he put his hand over Kirsten's on the table and gazed into her eyes. "That is, if she doesn't mind going with me."

Mind? She couldn't think of anything she would like better.

"I'd love to," she said softly, and turned her hand to squeeze his. "What shall I wear?"

The two women discussed wardrobes for a few minutes, and then the conversation turned to the Robertses. "We're practically newcomers in town," Dave told Kirsten with a grin. "We've only been here six years. We met while we were both working for the *Omaha World Herald*, but after the kids were born we decided the city was no place to raise them. We started looking around for a small-town paper to buy and finally settled here in Copper Canyon. We'll never get rich, but it's a great place to bring up children."

Kirsten felt a jolt of envy as she listened. "How many do you have?"

Sally answered. "Three. Two boys and a girl, ranging in age from eight to thirteen, and they love it here, too."

"You're so lucky," Kirsten said wistfully. "I adore babies. I'd like to have a house full of them."

She glanced covertly at Sam and noticed that he was frowning. Did he think she was hinting that she would like him to be the father? That hadn't been her intent, but if he thought so he obviously wasn't pleased by the idea. He'd told her he was going to remain a bachelor, so that must mean he didn't want his life cluttered up with youngsters, either.

No, Sam wasn't the type to father illegitimate babies and then walk away from them. He wouldn't be that irresponsible. And neither would she. Much as she would like to have him be the father of her children, she would never allow it unless they were married.

Kirsten's admission that she wanted children, lots of

them, startled Sam. When he'd been engaged to Belinda they'd seldom talked about having a family. He was too busy going to school and studying during those years to even take time out for a wedding. The last thing they'd needed was a child. Belinda had to work to help pay their rent and living expenses, and besides she'd never shown much interest in kids.

After she'd left him and married another man, he'd vowed never again to care enough for a woman to give her his heart or his trust, so there was no reason for him to think about having children of his own. That was simply out of the question.

But Kirsten was nothing like Belinda, so he shouldn't be surprised that she had strong maternal instincts. She would be a good mother.

That thought set up a vague yearning deep inside him, which he had no intention of exploring. In fact it was even more reason for him not to get involved with her. He didn't want to regret never having had children. He had his patients to take care of. That should satisfy any nagging paternal instinct that might surface now and then.

Sam knew he would forfeit anything to keep from hurting Kirsten as deeply as Belinda had hurt him. After the potluck supper he was going to strengthen his resolve not to see her again. In fact, he would tell her as much before he left the Buckley premises.

It was better to hurt her ego than to lead her on and run the risk of breaking her heart.

When the meal had been polished off, Coralie brought out the cake with all thirty-six of its candles lit. After numerous jokes about asking the fire department to stand by, Jim blew out the flames, everyone sang "Happy Birthday" and the dessert was cut and served with ice cream.

After everyone had eaten all they could, the tables were cleared and a stack of gaily wrapped presents was carried out and put on the table in front of Jim. The cards were humorous, but the gifts were useful and thoughtful.

By the time the last package was opened and the toasts were all drunk, it was after eight o'clock and the sun had gone down. The sky was beginning to darken when the sound of horses' hooves and wagon wheels attracted everyone's attention, just before two Clydesdale horses pulling a big wagon full of hay clip-clopped into the barnyard from the driveway.

Kirsten couldn't believe her eyes. She thought she'd been in on all the plans for the evening, but she hadn't known anything about this.

Jim looked as astonished as everyone else as the driver, who wore overalls and a straw cowboy hat, jumped down from the wooden seat high above the top of the four-sided wagon. He grinned as Coralie hurried over to him.

"Hey, guys," she called. "I've got a surprise for you. You all know Ike Turnbull here, who has the neighboring farm down the road. You've probably been on his hayrides before, but Kirsten and I are city girls and we've never had the pleasure. So in honor of Jim's birthday, and as a treat for Kirsten and me, Ike is going to take all of us for a ride. We'll leave in about ten minutes."

Everyone clapped, greeted Ike and headed for the house to get ready to leave. Kirsten turned to Sam, who was standing beside her. "I don't think Coralie told anyone about this. I didn't know."

Sam put his arm around her and started walking toward the house. "It'll be fun. I was a teenager last time I was on a hayride, but as I remember the darkness and the soft hay made it real convenient for making out."

"But these people are all married," she said.

"We're not," he murmured huskily, then hugged her briefly to his side and released her, leaving her weak-kneed and misty-eyed, as well as red-faced.

Sam was right. The hayride was fun, Kirsten thought an

hour later as the big wagonful of hay rumbled down the back county roads to the steady tattoo of the horses' hooves. Ike had supplied blankets for stretching out on, as well as cold beer and sodas, pretzels, chips and assorted nuts for munching. They sang songs and told stories, and as the night grew cooler, they snuggled up to their partners for warmth.

It was now totally dark with only a partial moon to light the way, which made it even more romantic. Sam and Kirsten cuddled together in the sweet-smelling hay with their blanket over them. They occupied a secluded corner of the wagon far enough away from the nearest neighboring couple to afford a modicum of privacy in the dark.

Sam had his arms around her, and her head was on his shoulder. "Are you enjoying this?" he asked softly as his lips brushed her hair.

Enjoying didn't even come close to describing the bliss she felt cradled in Sam's warm and tender embrace. "Ohh yes," she said on a ragged sigh as he moved his hand to cup her breast. "I wish it could go on forever."

He rolled her nipple between his two fingers. "You're not wearing a bra." His tone was unsteady.

She'd had misgivings when she was dressing, but now she was glad she hadn't worn a bra. "No, I'm not. The neckline of my blouse is so low and wide that my straps would have shown, so I left it off."

The neck of her blouse had elastic at the top of the wide ruffle, and he pulled it down then repositioned his hand under the material to stroke her bare breast. His fingers knew just how to touch her to make her melt under their caress.

"Are you deliberately trying to drive me out of my mind?" His voice was raw.

She turned slightly in his arms so she could reach up and rub her thumb over his lips. "I don't know," she admitted. "Maybe I am. Not consciously, but you're always so sure you can control your emotions no matter what the temptation, and I don't seem to have any restraint at all where you're concerned.''

While she'd been talking, he'd captured her thumb in his mouth and sucked greedily on it with a pull that went all the way to her core.

With a low groan his arms tightened around her and he encased her nude breast in his palm. ''Sweetheart, every time we're together I have to fight for control. I don't want to have to answer for what might happen when I lose the battle, and I will lose it if it goes on much longer.''

The idea of him wanting her so badly set her on fire. She wanted him just as much, and she wasn't nearly as inclined to fight it. She wished they were alone in this wagon instead of surrounded by people. Then she would find out whether or not he could hold out against her.

And why not? They were consenting adults. Why shouldn't they satisfy their mutual desire? It didn't have to lead to marriage. Probably by the time she was due to go back to California, they would be sated and realize it hadn't been the all-consuming passion of their lives, but just an overwhelming lust that had flared hot and then burned itself out.

Kirsten's breast in Sam's hand was soft and pliable, and he ached to take the hardened nipple in his mouth and suckle the nourishing sweetness of her. If only they were alone.

But if they were alone, they wouldn't be able to resist making love. Kirsten was as eager as he. The way she stroked his cheek and his throat with those soft, little hands, the mewling sounds that escaped from her throat as he caressed her breast, and the way her bent knee curled across his thigh told him that she was as hot as he was. If he gave in to his overwhelming need and made love to her when he took her home tonight, there would be no going back.

Kirsten wasn't the kind of woman men played games

with. She didn't know the rules. She played for keeps, even
though she might deny it in an effort to accommodate him.

No, he wasn't the type to deflower virgins. Not that she
was probably a virgin in the strict sense of the word, but
neither was she all that experienced. She was naive and
trusting, and he would never forgive himself if he breached
that trust.

But he couldn't put her away from him right now. After
all he was only human, and she was cooperating fully in
their harmless petting.

Harmless? Well, no, that wasn't altogether true. He knew
for sure that he would pay for it with a sleepless night of
frustration, and he suspected she would, too, but by morning they would both be cooled down and after that there
would be no more messing around.

Reluctantly he released her breast, then put his finger
under her chin to lift her face to his. He felt her cool breath
on his mouth just before he took hers. She put her arm
around his neck and parted her lips.

There was nothing chaste about this kiss, and he dropped
his hand to her bare thigh as their tongues mated. Her legs
were as soft and firm as they were beautiful and his finger
kneaded the silky flesh, raising goose bumps all over his
tough hide.

With a moan she slowly inched her knee upward until it
touched his throbbing groin. He clutched her leg and
pushed it harder against him as he struggled to swallow the
cry of exhilaration that rose unbidden in his throat.

Fortunately the wagon wheels hit a deep pothole in the
bumpy road just then and threw it enough off balance to
toss the passengers around in the hay. Sam and Kirsten
were wrested apart, and the disruption started everyone
talking again. By the time they got settled down, the Buckley farm loomed ahead and the trip was over.

Kirsten was both embarrassed and frustrated. What had
she been thinking of, making out so passionately with Sam

in the midst of all those people? True, it was dark and they were somewhat isolated from the others, but even so it was a tacky thing to do.

She'd never behaved like that before, but she didn't seem to have any inhibitions where Sam was concerned. She'd not only allowed the intimacy, she'd encouraged it!

They hadn't talked directly to each other since the incident, and as he helped her out of the wagon he didn't lift her down but touched only her hand to guide her. There seemed to be an invisible wall between them. Sam looked tight-lipped and disconcerted, and she was too discomfited to look him in the eye.

Before long the guests began taking their leave, and Sam sought her out. "When you're ready, I'll drive you over to the cottage."

"Thank you, but that won't be necessary," she assured him, not eager to prolong this uncomfortable situation. "I can walk."

"Not in the dark at this time of night," he said flatly, as if he were talking to a child.

She didn't argue, and as soon as the guests were all gone she picked up her purse and approached Jim and Coralie. "I don't think I've ever had a better time at a party," she told them, "and the hayride was a real treat. One I'll never forget."

Sam, who was standing beside her, was suddenly racked with a choking cough, and it was only then that she caught the double entendre. Well, she wasn't going to back down. Their hot petting session had made it even more unforgettable.

Once they finished their goodbyes, it took only seconds to drive from the big house to the cottage. Sam turned off the lights and the engine, then got out and came around the car to help her.

"You don't have to walk me to the door," she said as he took her arm. "I left the porch light on."

"I need to talk to you," he muttered.

Her heart pounded. Did that mean he wanted to come in? Maybe even spend the night? Heaven knows they'd been building up to just that before the pothole jolted them back to their senses.

They climbed the steps to the porch, and Kirsten unlocked the door, then turned to look at him. "Would you like to come in?" she asked hesitantly, afraid he might misunderstand and think she was coming on to him, the way he had the first time he brought her home.

On the other hand, she probably was. She sure wasn't going to say no if he wanted to finish what they'd started earlier.

"Yes, I want to come in," he answered gruffly. "I want to come in and make love to you so bad I can hardly stand it, but I'm not going to. I don't think you fully understand what you'd be letting yourself in for, if you gave yourself to me."

Her pulse sped up and the blood pounded in her head. He wanted her. He really wanted her, and it was all she could do not to throw herself into his arms and use every seductive trick she could think of to break down his resistance.

Instead she tried to slow down her breathing as she replied. "I'm not a child, Sam. I'm twenty-six years old and capable of making my own decisions. I know exactly what you want of me. You want a sex-only interlude that will end forever in two weeks when I leave Copper Canyon. It's not a very flattering offer and ordinarily I'd turn it down without hesitation, but you've been truthful with me. I've never known a man like you before."

He tried to speak but she hurried on. "I think I'm in love with you, but if I am it's my problem, not yours."

He shook his head, but again she continued without letting him interrupt. "I want you, Sam. I've never wanted a man as much as I want you, and if you'll make love with me I'll be going into it with my eyes wide open. No illusions or misunderstandings, and when it's time for me to leave, no recriminations.''

Sam leaned against the outside of the house and watched her. "Why are you willing to do this, Kirsten? Do you feel sorry for me because I'm so crazy for you? Or are you convinced that once we sleep together, I'll change my mind and ask you to marry me?''

Kirsten felt the twitch of a smile. The male ego was a vociferous thing. It never matured, but always needed to be fed with a woman's soft words and touch.

Well, she would nurture his ego, and she wouldn't have to lie.

"I want to make love with you even on your terms because I'm convinced that it could be the most explosive and earthshaking experience of my life, and I don't want to miss out just because there's no future in it.''

For a moment the silence between them was overpowering. Then he put his fist under her chin and tilted her head up so she had to look at him. "Are you sure?'' His voice was raspy.

She looked directly into his eyes and nodded. "Very sure.''

Tenderly he put his arms around her and drew her against him, then lowered his head and kissed her. She put her arms around his waist and cuddled closer. It was a gentle kiss, urgent but restrained, and she felt his body quicken in response, as did her own.

"Don't you think we should go inside?'' she murmured against his mouth. "A little privacy would be a nice change.''

He nuzzled her ear and she shivered. "Not tonight, sweetheart.'' She heard the strain in his voice. "I want to give you time to think about this. Will you come to my house for supper tomorrow night? We can make a final decision then.''

She was disappointed, but a tiny bit relieved, too. His hesitancy told her more than his words. He truly cared about her and didn't want to pressure her into going to bed with him just because they were both so aroused. He wanted her to be sure she knew what she was doing, and that made her even more certain that her decision was the right one.

Kirsten was too stirred up to sleep much that night, but even so when she woke the following morning she felt full of energy and eager to get on with the day.

Her first hurdle came at breakfast when she had to decide how much of what had gone on the previous night to tell Coralie. She finally concluded that the unvarnished truth was best. After all, Coralie was her best friend and hostess, and Kirsten trusted her implicitly.

She recounted her behavior with Sam during the hayride and afterward when he'd taken her home. Coralie listened wide-eyed and fully attentive to the very last word, but when Kirsten finished she was surprised to see that her friend was frowning.

"What?" Kirsten asked anxiously. "You don't approve? I promise we'll be discreet."

"It's not that," Coralie hurried to assure her. "It's just.. Kirsten, are you sure this is what you want to do? Sam isn't likely to change his mind about marriage, you know."

Kirsten relaxed. "I know that, and I accept it. He isn't seducing me, I'm seducing him. And I swear with God as my witness that I won't cause him any more pain."

Coralie brushed away that remark with a hand gesture. "It's not him I'm worried about, it's you. You're setting yourself up for a lifetime of heartache."

Kirsten opened her mouth, but Coralie wasn't about to relinquish the floor. "I know you. You're not the type for a limited short-term affair. You've admitted you're in love with him. If you sleep with him, you'll be even more deeply committed.''

Kirsten hadn't expected Coralie to argue with her about this, and now she wished she'd never told her. She didn't want to face reality. She wanted a few nights of bliss. If she was willing to accept the consequences, why not go for it?

"I have a feeling that I'm never going to love another man the way I love Sam," she explained, "and since I can't have him as a lifetime partner, I want these two weeks of happy memories. Is that too much to ask?"

Coralie shook her head sadly. "I don't know, Kirsten. That's a decision you'll have to make, but don't lose sight of the fact that those so-called 'happy' memories could come back to haunt you instead of brightening your lonely hours."

Kirsten resolutely shoved Coralie's warning out of her conscious mind and happily went about preparing for her tryst with Sam. She shampooed and set her hair, painted her finger- and toenails a bright red, and chose her prettiest matching flowered silk bra and bikini panties to inflame him when he removed the short flare-skirted dress that matched her nail polish.

She'd never been to Sam's house before, but found it easily with his directions and arrived on the stroke of six-thirty, the time he'd designated. His home was much bigger than she'd expected, and set on an even larger lot. She parked at the curb and walked up the cobblestone path to the front door.

Sam opened it on the first ring of the bell. He was wearing dark slacks and a white shirt and tie, but his feet were bare and his hair was damp and a little wild as though it recently had been toweled dry.

"I was watching for you and saw you drive up," he said as he stood aside to let her in. He closed the door after her, then took her in his arms and kissed her, long and hard. "Sorry," he murmured huskily, "but I couldn't wait. I've been looking forward to this all day."

"Don't apologize," she said, and ran her fingers through his tousled hair. "I've been waiting eagerly for it, too. Could I maybe have an encore of that greeting?"

He kissed her again, and this time they were both breathless when they finally came up for air. "Enough," he muttered unsteadily. "If we keep this up Esther's dinner will dry out in the oven."

"Who's Esther?" she asked as she nuzzled his neck.

"My part-time housekeeper," he answered, then took her by the shoulders and stepped back, breaking their embrace.

"Just give me a few minutes to finish dressing," he said as he turned and started up the stairway along the left wall. "Why don't you pour us a drink? The bar's in the family room, straight ahead to the living room and hang a right. You can't miss it."

He ran up the stairs and Kirsten found the family room. She'd fixed Sam a Scotch on the rocks and was looking for a bottle of vodka to make a screwdriver when the doorbell rang. She knew Sam was still upstairs, and she was only a couple of rooms from the entry hall so she decided to answer it.

She rushed across the living room and into the hall calling, "I'll get it," up the stairs as she headed for the door.

She pulled it open and found an attractive woman with a wide smile that lit her flawless face on the other side of the screen. She was a golden blonde, and her hair swirled around her bare shoulders. Her eyes were a deep piercing blue, and she wore a Hawaiian-print sarong that showed off her abundant curves to perfection.

The smile disappeared when she saw Kirsten, and her tone was cool when she spoke. "I've come to see Dr. Lawford."

Kirsten had to think fast. Now what did she do? If this was a patient she should have seen Sam at the office. He might not want his patients bothering him at home. But if she was a friend he would be upset if Kirsten didn't invite her in.

"I'll get him," she said. "May I tell him who's asking for him?"

The woman glared at her. "Tell him it's Belinda Evans. And don't worry, he'll see me."

Chapter Eight

The icy shock that gripped Kirsten sent chilling shivers racing through her body.

This was the woman Sam had loved so compulsively that she'd changed the whole course of his life when she betrayed him with another man.

But what was she doing here? According to local gossip, her parents still lived in Copper Canyon, but she hadn't been back since her wedding. She and her husband lived in Hawaii, and her mom and dad visited there frequently but she never came home.

Well, she was here now, and standing on Sam's doorstep demanding admittance.

The two women were still staring at each other when Sam's voice coming from behind Kirsten broke the silence and startled her. "Who is it, honey?" he asked and stepped up beside her.

For a fleeting moment he smiled at the visitor on the other side of the screen, then Kirsten watched as the blood drained from his face and his eyes widened with shock.

"Belinda!" The smile was gone and Kirsten actually felt

the jolt that rocked through him, causing his spine to stiffen and his hands to knot into fists.

"Hello, Sam," Belinda said in a low, throaty tone.

He drew in a shaky breath, and Kirsten could see that it was an effort for him to speak. "What are you doing here?"

His voice was rusty, as if he hadn't used it in a long time, and she felt an overwhelming urge to scratch the satisfied little smile off the face of the other woman.

Instead she dug her fingernails into her own palms as Belinda bit her pouty lip. "I...I've come home to stay with Mom and Dad," she said hesitantly. "Please, Sam, may I come in?"

He didn't answer but unlocked the screen door and pushed it open. Kirsten stepped back several paces, but Sam didn't move as Belinda walked into the entry hall, their gazes still locked, and then he pulled the screen shut behind her. She brushed lightly against him in the narrow space, and Kirsten cringed as though it were she who had been touched.

The woman was deliberately attempting to seduce him.

Neither of them seemed to notice Kirsten or remember she was there as Sam led the way into the living room with Belinda right behind him.

Kirsten's knees were trembling, and she leaned against the newel post of the stairway to steady herself. What was she supposed to do now? Obviously Sam's ex-fiancée wanted to talk to him alone, but she was the interloper. Kirsten was the one who had been invited, and she had no idea how Miss Manners would handle this situation.

The only thing she could do was follow her instincts, and they told her to find out what was going on even if it meant intruding where she was probably not welcome.

She pushed herself away from the support of the post and walked down the hall and into the living room. Belinda was sitting on the long, muted copper-colored damask sofa with her tanned bare legs crossed and the hem of her skirt almost to her lap. Sam had taken the flowered wing-backed chair at a right angle to the couch. Belinda looked up briefly as Kirsten walked in, then returned her full attention to Sam, but he showed no awareness of Kirsten's presence.

So much for her stupid daydream of overwhelming him with her charm and seductive ways so that he would forget all about his ex-lover, Ms. Belinda Evans—whatever her married name was.

Married name! Kirsten's legs nearly gave way, and she sank down onto a straight-backed chair against the wall opposite the sofa. Belinda Evans was married. So why didn't she use her husband's name? Where was this man whom she'd deserted Sam for?

The sound of Sam's voice interrupted Kirsten's thoughts. "Is something wrong with your parents, Belinda? If they've been sick, they haven't come to me for treatment—"

"Oh, no, it's nothing like that," she interrupted. "They're fine. It's me..." She paused dramatically and looked straight at Kirsten then back to him. "Could we... That is, could I talk to you alone?"

Sam turned to follow her gaze, and Kirsten knew from the look on his face that he'd forgotten she was even there. Quickly he rearranged his expression and stood. "Please forgive my lack of manners," he said. "Belinda, this is Kirsten Reinhold. Kirsten, Belinda Evans."

Without waiting for either woman to acknowledge the introduction, he put out his hand to Kirsten. "What are you doing over there?" he asked. "Come and join us."

She stood and Sam looked at Belinda. "I'm sorry, Belinda, but if you want to speak to me privately it will have to wait until tomorrow. As you can see I have a guest."

He took Kirsten's hand and seated her at the other end of the couch from Belinda, then returned to his chair.

The woman turned her head and looked at Kirsten pleasantly enough, but her blue eyes were cold and hard.

"Oh my, I'm afraid I misunderstood," she said to Sam. "I thought she was a student working part-time as household help. I mean, her being so young and all."

Kirsten's first impulse was to wipe that smirk off Belinda's face and deny that she was all that young and unsophisticated, but she managed to bite back the words before they tumbled out. That would just be playing into Belinda's trap. She knew the other woman was trying to put her on the defensive. Sam could defend himself if he wanted to, but Kirsten wasn't going to be lured into a catfight.

After all, when it came to women's ages, being young had it all over being middle-aged, and Belinda was Sam's age. Almost ten years older than Kirsten.

Sam frowned and started to get up. "I suggest you call me at the office tomorrow and—"

"No! Please!" Belinda interrupted. "If you don't mind me airing our dirty linen in front of Ms. Reinhold, it won't bother me. I really need to talk to you."

She sounded desperate, and Kirsten was inclined to believe that it wasn't an act. She probably didn't want to leave Kirsten and Sam alone together until she'd managed to recapture his undivided attention again.

He sank back into his chair. "And what dirty linen is that?" he asked tightly.

She folded her hands in her lap and looked down at them. "Please, Sam, don't be sarcastic. I assume she knows you and I were once lovers?" she asked softly, talking as though Kirsten wasn't there and making no attempt to include her in the conversation.

Sam nodded curtly. "She knows."

Belinda looked disappointed, as though she'd expected to get a reaction from Kirsten who was clenching her jaw to keep from doing just that. At the very least his ex-fiancée was trying to provoke a childish display of temper.

Again Belinda lowered her eyes. "I...I've left Greg and

filed for divorce,'' she said huskily, and immediately she had Sam's full attention.

He stared at her as she continued. ''Our marriage was a terrible mistake, Sam. I've paid many times over for what I did to you....''

She paused and rubbed her eyelids with her fingertips. ''I know you hate me—'' She bit her lip and wrung her hands.

Sam wiped his palm over his face. ''I don't hate you, Belinda,'' he said raggedly.

''If you don't, then you're a better man than most,'' she replied, and Kirsten was certain she'd rehearsed this little speech to wring all the emotion she could out of it. ''What I did was unforgivable, but I was young and totally self-centered at the time.'' She sniffled and reached in her purse for a tissue. ''I...I hope we can at least be friends now that I'll be living in town again.''

Sam didn't answer, but got up and walked over to the fireplace and turned his back to her as he gazed into the empty grate. His expression was stony, and he'd jammed his fists into his pockets. It was all Kirsten could do not to go to him, put her arms around him and try to ease his anguish.

But she couldn't do that. It wasn't her he wanted. He was only vaguely aware that she was there.

How could Belinda be so cruel? The least she could have done was prepare him for her return. She should have written to tell him about her divorce and her plan to come back to Copper Canyon, then asked to see him.

But no. Not this conniving witch. That wouldn't have been dramatic enough. She couldn't resist turning the knife in Sam a few more times just to prove she could still taunt him while she was seducing him.

Again he spoke and interrupted Kirsten's thoughts. ''There's no reason why we can't live in the same town without being either friends or foes. I'm sure we can be polite to each other—"

A loud sob brought Belinda to her feet. "You see," she said as she walked toward him with tears streaming down her cheeks. "You...you do hate me."

He turned to face her and she walked right into his arms.

Kirsten felt as if she'd been hit in the stomach. A wave of nausea washed through her, and she rose and hurried out the front door, but not before she saw Belinda looking at her over Sam's shoulder, a light of triumph in her eyes.

Kirsten sped down the highway in the opposite direction from the farm. She couldn't go back there. It was too early. Coralie would see Kirsten drive in and want to know what had happened, why she was home before she and Sam had even had time to eat, and she wasn't up to talking about it. She wasn't sure she ever would be.

Too upset to even think, let alone pay attention to where she was going, she just drove around turning this way and that on the twisting and climbing rural roads until she realized she was thoroughly lost. Not only that, but she was well up into the mountains where towns were few and far between, her gas was getting low and it was almost dark.

For the first time in hours her grief was overridden by another emotion, panic. She could get caught all alone in these unfamiliar mountains and have to spend the night with God only knew what wild animals prowling around. If there were bears, she knew they sometimes got into cars, and mountain lions couldn't be ruled out, either.

She shivered with fear and started looking for signs of life. There must be cabins up here, she thought. A lot of people had summer homes in the mountains. Maybe there were even public telephones in some places beside the road.

After about ten minutes she finally spotted the lights of a cabin through the trees, and breathed a sigh of relief. As she drew closer, she noticed a rural mailbox on a pole at the side of a driveway that led to the lights. She turned in and parked in back of the rather beat-up pickup that was already there.

After turning off the engine, she hesitated before getting out. She knew that seeking admittance to a strange house in the middle of the night could be dangerous. What if there was a man, or men inside, who thought rape was an indoor sport? She wouldn't stand much chance of getting away from them. But she wouldn't have any chance of defending herself against a bear or mountain lion.

She took a deep breath, picked up her purse and opened the door.

It was pretty rugged terrain and the lights inside the cabin did little to illuminate the pitch-blackness outside. To complicate matters she was wearing spike-heeled pumps, but by being careful how and where she walked she made it to the steps and the supporting railing that led up to the front porch. It was a rustic but solidly built structure, and she pounded on the heavy door.

She heard a rustling from inside, then the porch light went on and a man's voice called, "Jerry? Is that you?"

Before she could answer he pulled open the door and stood silhouetted in the light wearing cutoff jeans and a faded plaid shirt. "Where the hell have you been, fella? I caught four trout while I was waiting—"

He stopped abruptly and stared. "You're not Jerry," he accused, then did a double take. "Kirsten? Kirsten Reinhold? Where did you come from?"

She blinked. Then blinked again. It was Don Sterling, the insurance broker who had taken her to his brother and sister-in-law's barbecue.

"Don!" she exclaimed. "Yes, it's me, but what are you doing here? Is this your cabin?"

"Yeah," he said as he opened the door to admit her. "That is, it belongs to the family. Come on in. Is something wrong? We don't have a phone. Did someone send you here with a message?''

She was so relieved that she laughed at the absurdity of that last question as she stepped inside. "No, nobody sent me, I was out driving and got lost. Yours were the only lights I saw, so I took a chance. Am I interrupting anything?''

Now it was his turn to laugh. "If you mean a tryst with a beautiful woman, you've got to be kidding. No lady would put up with me lookin' like this.''

He held out his arms to his sides and circled around. "I've been wading the creek all afternoon and haven't bothered to shower and shave yet. Also, I smell like fish.''

She wrinkled her nose. "I noticed," she said wryly. "You say you caught four trout?''

"Sure did," he answered proudly. "I was just about to fry them. Will you join me for a late supper?''

It occurred to her that she hadn't had anything to eat since noon. Belinda was probably sharing the dinner Sam's housekeeper had prepared for him.

"Well, I...I was hoping you could give me directions back to the main road. I want to get home as soon as possible. I don't like driving around in these woods at night.''

Don shook his head. "Sorry, but you'd never find your way in the dark. I'm afraid you're stuck here until morning. But hey, you're more than welcome. Just give me a few minutes to shower and change clothes, and then I'll fix us something to eat.''

Kirsten gasped. "Oh, I can't do that. I mean, you...you don't have enough space...'' Her voice trailed off as she gazed around the small interior.

The cabin consisted of two rooms: a combination kitchen, dining and living room, and near the back wall was a door that was opened into a bedroom. There must be a bathroom back there, too, she surmised, since he'd mentioned taking a shower.

"Sure there is," Don assured her. "You can have the bedroom and I'll sleep on the sofa."

Kirsten wasn't convinced. "But you're expecting another man. Jerry someone?"

Don chuckled. "Don't let him worry you. He's a pal of mine who said he might come up today for some fishing, but he would have been here long ago if he were coming."

Don shrugged. "And even if he should come, this sofa opens into a double bed."

He sobered and looked at her. "Are you afraid I might have something in mind other than sleeping?" he asked softly. "You're right to be suspicious of any man you don't know well, but I swear I'd never force myself on you or hurt you in any way. I guess you'll just have to take my word for it, though, because there's no lock on the bedroom door."

Fear had been uppermost in her mind, as a matter of fact. She would have been incredibly stupid not to be wary, even though Don wasn't exactly a stranger. She'd dated him, met members of his family and seen how well liked he was by the people in the community, but even so that was no guarantee.

On the other hand, she really didn't have a choice. She would never find her way out of these woods, when she couldn't even see the road. Besides, her gut instinct told her Don was just as nice as he seemed to be.

She smiled. "I trust you, Don, and I appreciate your invitation. To prove it I'll even cook for you while you're in the shower. Just point me to the food."

"Great!" he said, then frowned. "But you can't cook in that outfit. If you splatter grease on that dress it will be ruined."

She glanced down at her clothes, having forgotten all about how she was dressed. "The dress can be easily dry-cleaned," she assured him, "but if you have an extra pair of heavy socks I can wear I'd like to get out of these shoes.''

''Sure thing,'' he said, then hesitated. ''Kirsten, I don't mean to pry, but would you mind telling me what you're doing way out here in the middle of nowhere, and all dressed up like you were going to a party?''

Kirsten didn't want to talk about what had happened, but she owed Don an explanation. The pain that had temporarily receded came back, but she took a deep breath and dived in.

''I had a date to go out this evening. We were going to have dinner at his house, and I... Well, I wanted to look nice so I dressed up a little. I'd only been there a few minutes when...'' She didn't want to use names. In a village the size of Copper Canyon the gossip would be all over town within hours, but she couldn't be explicit about what happened either or everyone would know she was talking about Sam and Belinda.

''We quarreled,'' she began, improvising, ''and I was so upset that I left and just started driving—''

''Did he hit on you?'' Don demanded. ''Tell me who it was and I'll—''

''No! No, it was nothing like that!'' Oh damn! Now what was she going to say?

''We...we didn't exactly quarrel. There was an outside intrusion that upset me. Anyway, I wasn't paying attention to where I was driving until it got dark, and then I didn't know where I was.''

She grimaced. ''It isn't the smartest thing I've ever done.''

Don reached out and patted her shoulder. ''Don't be too hard on yourself. Something pretty bad must have happened to make you react so strongly. Is there anything I can do?''

The corners of Kirsten's mouth turned up in a small smile. ''You've already done it. You've offered me food and shelter. What more could I ask of you? Thank you, Don. You're a nice man.''

He looked pleased, but when he spoke his tone was grim. "Don't let any of the rednecks around here upset you. You can always come to me if you have a problem."

He still didn't get the picture, but his offer made her feel warm and cared for. "It looks like that's exactly what I've done," she said huskily, "and I appreciate your generosity."

Her eyes were beginning to mist, and she quickly changed the subject. "Now, you go clean up while I tackle those trout."

Kirsten was exhausted and slept through the night in Don's rather lumpy bed without waking. She'd tried to get him to let her take the couch, but he wouldn't hear of it and instead stretched out on it himself.

She didn't wake until almost nine o'clock, and Don insisted she have some breakfast before she left. Then she had to stop for gas at the first filling station she came to, so now it was noon and she was just approaching the outskirts of Copper Canyon. Another twenty minutes and she would be home.

Instinctively, she slowed down. She wasn't looking forward to facing Coralie. Not that her friend would be worried about her. Both she and Coralie had expected that she would stay the night with Sam, but Coralie would be excited and want to hear all about it. Well, that is, *almost* all about it. After all, there were some things a girl didn't even share with her best friend!

The ache of defeat washed over Kirsten. She wouldn't be sharing glad tidings with Coralie because there were no glad tidings to share. She felt like such a fool.

Pressing her foot on the gas pedal again, she accelerated. She might as well get this over with and start making plans to go back to California. By the time the day was over everyone in town would know that Dr. Sam and his Belinda were back together again, and Kirsten didn't want to be around to hear about it.

As she turned into the driveway to the house she was appalled to see Sam's white BMW parked in the barnyard, and Sam and Coralie standing beside it talking. Damn! He probably hadn't been able to wait to tell Jim and Coralie that Belinda was back, and that he was happily giving her a shot at tearing his heart out a second time.

Kirsten would have backed her car out and driven on past, but just then they looked up and saw her. Coralie waved somewhat frantically and started to run toward her, but Sam stood where he was and waited for her to come to him. Unless she wanted to appear to be running away, she had no choice but to do just that.

She eased her vehicle up to park beside the BMW and cut the engine. Sam, looking like the god of thunder, stomped over and opened her door. "Where in hell have you been all night?" he bellowed.

She was so taken aback that she could only stare at him as she climbed out of her car. What was his problem? And what business was it of his where she'd been?

"Have you any idea how worried we've been?" he ranted. "Didn't it even occur to you to at least let Coralie know where you were?"

Kirsten felt the heat rising in her, and this time it was definitely not passion. It was pure rage.

"Now just a damn minute," she grated between clenched jaws. "Since when do I have to account to you for my whereabouts? You sure weren't giving me a second thought the last time I saw you."

He had the grace to look ashamed. "No, I wasn't," he said quietly, "and I'm sorry. My behavior was abominable, but I was so shocked—"

His cold fury was gone, and he looked at her through eyes dark with pain and frustration. Her rage cooled, too, but she wasn't willing to let him blame her for any discomfort her actions last night might have caused him.

"Of course you were," she said reasonably. "I understand that, but what are you so upset about now?"

He glared at her. "Why wouldn't I be?" he demanded. "You left my house without saying a word to anybody and didn't come back there or here all night. It's now…" He looked at his watch. "Past noon and we've been going crazy all morning. We were just about to call the police—"

Kirsten's eyes widened and her voice elevated. "The police! You were going to call the police! What gives you the right to check up on me?"

"I was worried, damn it!" he interrupted. "I was afraid you'd had an accident or gotten lost, or mugged, or abducted—"

"Abducted?" she said sarcastically.

"It's been known to happen," he reminded her.

"Not to me it hasn't. Darn it, Sam, I'm twenty-six years old. Old enough to vote, drink alcohol, run for public office, and even stay out all night occasionally."

She drew a deep breath, then asked, "Did Belinda spend the night with you?"

As soon as the words were out, she knew they were a low blow and strictly none of her business, but it was too late to take them back.

He looked startled. "No, she didn't," he said grimly. "Adultery is one sin I've never indulged in. I'm sorry you didn't know that without asking."

An unwelcome feeling of shame welled in Kirsten, making her all the angrier. How was she supposed to know what his habits were? He hadn't let her get close enough to find out.

"She told you she was getting a divorce," Kirsten blustered.

Before Sam could answer Coralie's voice broke into the argument, jolting them both. Kirsten had forgotten she was there, and apparently so had Sam. They both turned to look at her.

"Kirsten, are you all right?" she asked anxiously. "I didn't realize you hadn't come home last night until Sam called this morning thinking you were with me since you didn't answer your phone at the cottage. He explained that you weren't with him either and..."

Her words trailed off and she looked beseechingly at Kirsten. "I don't mean to pry, but..."

Those were the same words Don had used the night before when he'd questioned her, and she realized that neither of them was prying. They had a legitimate concern and a need to know.

She reached out and hugged Coralie, then released her. "I'm sorry, Coralie, but we'd talked yesterday and I thought you wouldn't worry about me."

What she meant was she'd told her friend yesterday that she would probably be spending the night with Sam so if she didn't come home Coralie wasn't to worry, but she didn't want to come right out and say that in front of him. The whole thing was too embarrassing as it was.

She couldn't bear it if Sam found out that she'd been so sure he would want her to make love with him, when in fact he'd more or less ignored her once Belinda appeared on the scene.

Coralie understood and worded her answer carefully. "I didn't until Sam called this morning, but if you were way-laid and held somewhere against your will last night... Well, both Sam and I want to know about it."

Again Kirsten felt torn. She did owe them an explanation, but she wasn't going to admit how badly Belinda's unexpected appearance and Sam's response to it had upset her. She needed to preserve at least a little of her shattered pride.

"I...I'm really sorry that I've caused you so much anxiety," she said, speaking directly to Coralie. "I gather Sam has told you that Belinda Evans is back?"

Coralie's mouth tightened into a thin white line of disapproval. "Yes, he has," she said, and Kirsten cringed at the pity she saw in her friend's eyes. She hated being the object of such a demeaning emotion, and it firmed her resolve not to tell the whole truth about how devastated she'd been by Belinda's return and Sam's reaction to her.

She took a deep breath and plunged ahead. "Well, it was pretty obvious that they didn't even remember I was there..." Sam made a half moan, half strangling noise, but Kirsten paid no attention. "So after a while I just left. I mean, there really wasn't much of anything else I could do."

Sam looked as if he was going to interrupt, so she hurried on, feeling out the story as she went along. "I didn't want to come back here. It was early and I was upset, so I just started driving around. I wasn't paying attention to where I was going and I got lost."

She hesitated, not sure where this was leading. She wanted to stick as close to the truth as possible so she wouldn't get too tangled up in lies.

"By then it was dark and I panicked," she continued. "After all, I live on the seashore. I'm not used to the tricky art of driving on the winding roads in the incredible darkness of an unfamiliar mountain forest."

Sam looked troubled. "Good Lord, you didn't spend the night in the car, did you?"

"No," she hastened to assure him, happy that she wasn't having to lie after all. The truth seemed to work fine as long as she kept any emotion out of the story. "Fortunately, I finally saw the lights of a cabin and turned in there."

This time Sam frowned. "You sought help in the middle of the night from strangers in a cabin?" He sounded disapproving.

"What else could I do?" she bristled. "It was the only

place around, and I didn't relish being mauled by bears or mountain lions. But wait until I tell you. The cabin belonged to Don Sterling! He was up there to do some fishing. Isn't that a coincidence?''

Sam's eyebrows twitched. "Who was with him?"

"Oh, he was alone," Kirsten said innocently, too buoyed by the ease with which her story flowed to notice the suspicion in Sam's tone. "One of his buddies was supposed to come up, but he never got there."

"How convenient," Sam said grimly. "Did Don give you directions to the nearest motel where you could spend the night?"

The coldness in his tone chilled even Kirsten and she blinked. "No, he didn't. It was too late and too dark to go out. He invited me to stay there. You have some objection to that?" she asked bitingly.

"Damn right I have," he snarled. "What kind of naive idiot do you think I am? Hasn't it occurred to you that you're straining your credibility a bit far by expecting me to believe that you *just happened* to be driving around, and *just happened* to get lost and the only cabin you saw *just happened* to belong to a man you've been dating? Come on, give me a break. You knew exactly where you were going, didn't you? Did you sleep with him?''

She heard Coralie gasp, but was too infuriated to appreciate her friend's outrage at his question. Who was he to make assumptions like that about her? He'd been holding another man's wife in his arms when she last saw him!

Making a massive effort to calm down and control her voice, she looked right at him and smiled. "I'm afraid we didn't get a whole lot of sleep," she said huskily, "but yes, I did spend the night with him."

Chapter Nine

Kirsten's admission slammed into Sam like a blow to the solar plexus, and he put his arm across his stomach and tilted forward slightly to help assuage the pain.

Was she telling the truth? Had she so casually spent last night making love with Don Sterling? He'd never known her to lie, but then she could have been stringing him along all this time and he wouldn't have suspected. He really didn't know her well enough to tell if she was lying or not.

He couldn't seem to wrest his gaze away from her. She looked so young and innocent with her creamy, unblemished complexion and cap of dark, curly hair.

If she wasn't telling the truth she was an excellent actress. Her wide brown eyes caught his gaze and held it, indicating that she had nothing to hide, and he felt sick.

With a muttered oath he spun around and got in his car. After fumbling for a few seconds to find his keys, he jammed one in the ignition and started the engine.

Apparently she was another Belinda. When was he going to learn that women couldn't be trusted?

He shifted into Reverse, backed the car around and

roared out of the driveway and onto the highway without even hearing the loud screech of his obscenely expensive tires.

Kirsten and Coralie watched from the barnyard as Sam's Beemer disappeared from view in a cloud of dust down the graveled country highway.

Coralie turned to Kirsten and glared at her. "Why did you lie to Sam?"

Kirsten blinked with surprise. "What makes you think I lied?"

"Because I know you too well," Coralie said as she turned and started walking toward the house. "You wouldn't have recreational sex with any man. Now tell me what really happened so we can find a way to straighten things out with Sam."

Kirsten walked beside her. "Everything I told him was the truth. I just left a few things out and phrased others to imply what I wanted him to believe."

Coralie looked confused, but Kirsten hurried on. "I'm not interested in straightening things out with him," she said firmly, "but I do want to apologize to you. I'm cutting my vacation short. I'm going back to Eureka tomorrow or the next day, but since I've been a guest in your home you'll have to endure any gossip that might go around."

"You mean you're going to turn tail and run away without even putting up a fight for the man you love?" Coralie taunted. "If so, you're not the Kirsten Reinhold I've known and admired."

Kirsten felt a sharp stab of betrayal as they climbed the stairs to the porch. How could her best friend not understand?

"Yes, I am, if that's the way you insist on putting it," she said firmly. "I'm sorry if I'm disappointing you, but I'm not into embracing unwinnable causes."

Coralie opened the door and they walked into the living

room. "Sam told me from the very beginning that he'd had a disastrous love affair and wasn't going to put himself into a position to get burned like that again," Kirsten continued. "I knew he wasn't going to fall in love and marry me, but stupid as I am, I thought I could change his mind. Now that Belinda's come back I'm not going to make a spectacle of myself by sticking around and embarrassing all three of us."

Coralie sighed and changed the subject. "Look, we've finished dinner, but there's plenty left. Let's go in the kitchen and I'll warm it up for you. You can eat while we talk."

"I'm not hungry," Kirsten told her. "Don fixed me a late breakfast—"

Coralie turned and looked at her, surprise evident in her expression. "Then you really did spend the night with him?"

Kirsten nodded. "Yes, I did, but we had separate beds in separate rooms. He never touched me or made suggestive remarks."

As if by mutual agreement they walked over to the sofa and sat down. "Jim's out in the fields and Gloria and Amber are spending the day with friends," Coralie said, "so we have the house to ourselves. Feel free to say whatever you want to."

The adrenaline had stopped pumping and Kirsten suddenly felt drained and ashamed. "I'm afraid I've already done that," she said sadly. "I had no right to blow up at Sam that way. After all, he was concerned about me."

"That's putting it mildly," Coralie muttered. "He was frantic when I told him you hadn't come home last night, and so was I when I learned that you weren't with him. You'd said—"

"I know what I said," she interrupted quietly. "I told you I'd probably spend the night with him, and I would have, too, if he'd asked me. Thank God Belinda showed up before we got to that stage.''

She shuddered and felt the hot flush of humiliation at the thought of what the woman might have walked in on if she'd shown up later in the evening.

Coralie nodded. "Sam told me she arrived just a few minutes after you did, but he was pretty vague about what happened after that. Cut him a little slack, Kirsten. He was shocked out of his mind when he saw her standing on his doorstep.''

This time it was Kirsten's turn to nod. "I know that, but I hope you'll give me a little credit, too. Her appearance and his reaction just about devastated me.''

"I don't doubt that,'' Coralie said with genuine understanding, "so start right there and tell me everything that happened after that.''

Kirsten did. The words tumbled out as she relived the disappointment, humiliation and anguish of the night before. The telling was both an agony and a catharsis, as she described her shattered dreams when Belinda walked so confidently back into Sam's life; her anger at Sam's apparent total indifference to her after that; her fear when she realized she was lost in the forest; and her gratitude to Don for taking her in and treating her like a valued friend instead of a plaything.

By the time Kirsten finished tears were streaming down her face, and Coralie handed her a box of tissues from the end table. "I'm sorry you and Sam were so worried about me,'' she said on a sob. "That was never my intention. There was no phone in the cabin or I would have called you as soon as I woke up.''

"It wasn't your fault,'' Coralie said sympathetically. "Sam said that when he discovered you were gone he tried to phone you at the cottage several times but no one answered. He figured you just weren't answering your phone, and he couldn't blame you for not wanting to speak to him so he waited until early this morning and called us. That was when we found out that you hadn't come home last night. The poor guy was nearly crazy and so were Jim and I.''

Kirsten ran her hands through her soft, curly hair. ''I guess I really screwed up this time, didn't I? But then, it'll be the last time he ever gives me a second thought. From now on he'll have his beloved Belinda to make life hell for him.''

''Aren't you jumping to conclusions?'' Coralie asked testily.

Kirsten sighed. ''You're right, I probably am. I'm not exactly impartial, you know. Maybe she truly is repentant and will work hard at being a good wife for him.''

''I'm not talking about Belinda,'' Coralie snapped. ''I'm talking about you. I can guarantee he's going to give you a lot of thought. Why did you deliberately let him think you'd made love with Don Sterling?''

Kirsten spread her hands in an expressive gesture. ''Don't you see? I couldn't let him know how agonizing Belinda's return was for me. I do have some pride. He's never led me on in any way. He wouldn't even make love with me the night before last, when we were both so hot we could hardly resist. He wanted to give me more time to think about it and decide if a short but passionate affair with him was really what I wanted. The only promise he ever made to me was that whatever developed between us would be over once I left here.''

She jammed her finger in her chest. ''*I* was the one who fell in love. *I* was the one with the king-size ego who was so sure I could succeed where all the other women who were attracted to him had failed. *I* was the heroine who would charm him into forgetting all about his first love and falling wildly, passionately, deeply in love with me.''

She sniffled and wiped her wet cheeks with the back of her hand. ''I don't want Sam to feel guilty for something he didn't do. It wasn't his fault I fell in love with him. I got myself tangled in that quagmire, and I'll get myself out of it. The best way to do that is to get the hell out of here and go back to California and to work.

"I'd like to leave in the morning, but I've got to have the car checked out first. It tended to stall every time I had to stop this morning, while I was driving down the mountain. I probably won't be able to get away until the day after tomorrow, if that's okay with you."

Coralie put her arms around Kirsten and held her. "Honey, I don't want you to leave a minute earlier than you have to, but if this is what you want to do I'll help in any way I can."

The rest of the day went by in a dull haze. Kirsten did her laundry and started packing the clothes she wouldn't need for the next couple of days, but she couldn't seem to work up any energy. The subject of her disappearance the night before and her plans to leave earlier than she'd originally intended were not discussed at the supper table. Coralie had briefed Jim privately, and none of them wanted to talk in front of the girls.

Kirsten excused herself shortly after helping clean up the kitchen, pleading exhaustion, which was true. She felt as if she'd been jogging for miles, although she hadn't been active at all. It was probably the trip to and from the mountains that had done her in. She'd lived all her life at sea level, and the change in altitude was very likely getting to her.

Copper Canyon's three-thousand-plus feet hadn't bothered her, but the other two thousand feet or so in the mountains could easily be the cause of her fatigue.

She went to bed early, and woke the next morning feeling better but still not very energetic. Pulling on her jeans and T-shirt, she didn't bother with makeup except for a touch of lipstick.

After breakfast at the big house she called Jackson and Son's Garage and made an appointment to take her car in at ten o'clock. Coralie followed in the Jeep, and the two planned to do some shopping while Butch Jackson put Kirsten's vehicle in tip-top shape for the long drive to Eureka.

They were selecting staples in the town's only supermarket when they turned a corner and ran smack into a grocery cart coming down the aisle from the opposite direction.

"Oh, I'm sorry," Kirsten, who was pushing the cart, said as she looked up and straight into the gaze of Belinda Evans.

Oh God, just what she needed! Another tussle with Sam's true love. And wouldn't you know, she was impeccably dressed in a blue tailored pantsuit and full makeup, while Kirsten knew she looked like a farmhand just in from the back forty.

"Well, if it isn't Ms. Kirsten," Belinda said dryly. "Sorry, but I've forgotten your last name."

Kirsten girded herself for another battle of insults. "That's all right," she said coolly. "I never knew yours. Your *married* name, that is."

The other woman flushed slightly but didn't miss a beat. "It's unimportant now that we're divorcing."

Belinda looked at Coralie. "And you must be Jim Buckley's new wife. I knew Marsha, his first wife. She was a love. She, Jim, Sam and I all grew up together."

She paused for a moment. "I understand you were a mail-order bride." There was an unmistakable note of disdain in her tone.

Kirsten's hands gripped the cart handle. She could hold her own with this witch, but she wasn't going to let her cut Coralie to ribbons with her tongue.

However, before she could protest, Coralie proved that she was also a match for Belinda. "Yes," she said sweetly.

"Isn't it amazing the things that go through the mail nowadays?"

Without hesitation Coralie put out her hand in a friendly gesture, as if she wasn't aware of the thick fog of antagonism that hovered around them. "I'm Coralie Buckley, and you must be Belinda Evans. I've heard so-o-o much about you."

Her tone was still sweetly innocent, but there was a faint undertone to that last sentence implying that what she'd heard wasn't all that flattering.

Belinda's expression hardened. She ignored Coralie's extended hand and turned to Kirsten. "Sam tells me you're just visiting the Buckleys from California and will be leaving us any day now."

That hurt, but Kirsten refused to let it show. She hated it that Sam had been talking about her to Belinda. What else had he told her? Had they laughed about the fact that Kirsten had admitted she was falling in love with him?

"Yes, I am," she said, managing to keep her voice calm. "I'm a nurse and have to get back to work."

She couldn't resist letting her opponent know that she was college-educated, too, and held an important job.

"Oh yes, Sam told me that, also," the other woman said slyly. "You know, of course, that he's used to having nurses fall in love with him."

Kirsten was too stunned to answer, but Coralie saved the day. Gently she pushed Kirsten out of the way and grabbed the cart. "Yes, well, not that it hasn't been fun talking to you, but we country girls have to get back to the farm," she said gaily. "It's time to muck out the stalls and slop the hogs. Stop in anytime. We can always use some help with the manure."

She steered her cart around Belinda's and together she and Kirsten marched up the aisle to the checkout counter.

Kirsten fumed on the way back to the garage, but had herself under control by the time they got there. Butch was waiting for them. "Sorry, Miss Reinhold," he said as he wiped his oil-stained hands on a grayish towel, "but you got more trouble than I thought. There's a problem with the computer in your car. It's gonna have to be replaced, and no one around here keeps 'em in stock. It'll take a few days for me to get one and put it in, and since we're not open on weekends it'll probably be Monday before I can get it back to you."

"Oh no!" Kirsten groaned. "I was planning to leave for California tomorrow morning!" Now what was she going to do?

"'Fraid you can't do that," Butch muttered sympathetically. "You don't want to start out on a trip in a car that has computer problems like this one's. You'd get stuck in the boonies."

"He's right," Coralie agreed. "You'd be crazy to drive that car anywhere until it's fixed. A delay in leaving is no great tragedy. You've still got over a week left before you're scheduled to return to work."

Kirsten's shoulders slumped and she sighed. "I suppose not, but I'd gotten myself all psyched up to leave and now..."

She let the rest of the sentence die. "How much will all this cost?" she asked Butch, and wondered if she had enough credit on her card to cover it.

"Come back to the office with me and I'll figure it up," he replied. "If you bought the car new, it might still be covered by the warranty."

Kirsten shook her head in defeat. "I bought it second-hand and didn't buy an extended warranty. The last thing I expected to have trouble with was the computer."

Butch clucked. "Them little suckers are great when they work, and a big pain in the backside when they don't."

Half an hour later Kirsten was riding back to the farm in the Jeep with Coralie after leaving behind her car and the prospect of a several-hundred-dollar debit on her credit card.

That night she went to bed early again. She couldn't understand why she'd been so tired the past couple of days, but chalked it up to the emotional roller coaster she'd been on. First the shock of Belinda's unexpected appearance, and then the disappointment and added expense with the car.

She would be glad to get home and back to work!

The following morning Kirsten woke up coughing and wheezing, and it was then that she finally realized her problem wasn't altitude but asthma. Some nurse she was! Didn't recognize the symptoms of asthma, even though she'd only recently recovered from a severe attack of the nasty stuff.

Thank heaven now that she knew what it was she could treat it. She had her medication and bronchial dilator with her. Once she started giving herself a treatment four times a day as prescribed, her bronchial tubes would clear up and she would be full of vim and vigor again.

Climbing out of bed, she gathered up the necessary equipment and inhaled the medicine. Almost immediately she was breathing more easily. Everything should be okay now, she thought. Just as a precaution she really should be checked by a doctor, especially since she would be starting a long trip in a few days, but Sam was the only one available and no way was she going to him.

The very thought of stripping to the waist for him and feeling his strong, competent hands on her bare flesh almost brought on another fit of coughing.

Asthmatic attacks were often induced by stress, and she'd had plenty of that lately. Once she got back home she would make an appointment to see her own physician. Meanwhile, she wasn't going to mention this to anybody, not even Coralie. She didn't want people hovering over her. She just wanted to try to enjoy the rest of her time at the farm.

The next day was Friday, and Kirsten spent her time helping Coralie can tomatoes. Since both of them were city girls, the possibility of them having to know how to can anything had never crossed their minds until Jim had come into the kitchen the day before carrying a bushel basket of ripe red tomatoes.

"These are going to spoil if they aren't canned within the next day or two," he'd announced, much to the dismay of his wife.

"But...but I don't know how to can vegetables," Coralie had stammered. "Can't I freeze them?"

Jim had smiled with amusement. "Honey, you can't freeze tomatoes. They have to be canned. You either do them whole or make sauce. Get Gloria to help you. She knows how."

Gloria was less than enthusiastic, but early this morning the three of them had turned the kitchen into a cannery with big kettles of boiling glass jars and huge vats of tomatoes, both whole and sauce.

Jim checked in from time to time to make sure no one had been cut by exploding jars or spilled boiling hot tomatoes on themselves. By late afternoon they were finally finished and had neat rows of canned tomatoes and sauce lined up on the counter.

When Jim came in for supper he was delighted. His face broke into a big grin and he scooped his wife up in his arms and gave her a sizzling kiss.

"You see, sweetheart," he said breathlessly, "that wasn't so bad, was it?"

Coralie nuzzled his neck, then smiled sweetly. "I have just one thing to say to you, my darling," she said huskily. "If you have anything else in that garden that's going to need to be canned, I want it plowed under immediately. And next year if you stick a tomato plant in the ground anywhere on this property you can damn well can it yourself."

He hooted with laughter and put her down. "That's my girl," he said affectionately. "Speak up and say what's on your mind."

He gave her a loving pat on the tush, then held up his right hand. "I swear with God as my witness that you will never have to can another vegetable or fruit." He winked at her and put his hand down. "On the other hand, how about freezing them?"

She muttered a little teasing yowl and wound up back in his arms again.

Kirsten felt tears welling in her eyes. It was beautiful to see how much Jim and Coralie loved each other. If only... If only... But there were no "if onlys" for Kirsten. She'd shattered any small hope of a love like that for herself when she'd led Sam to believe she'd spent a night making love with another man.

Both women and Gloria were exhausted by the time supper was over, and Jim assigned Amber to do the dishes while Kirsten collapsed on the couch and Coralie settled down in her thickly padded recliner.

They were watching the news on television and Jim had gone out to do the nightly chores, when the phone rang in the kitchen. Amber answered it and after a few seconds called out, "It's for you, Kirsten. Dr. Sam."

Kirsten's whole body jerked and brought her to an upright position before she even had time to think.

"For me?" she said stupidly. "Sam wants to talk to me?"

Her heart was pounding and she wasn't sure if it was with delight or fear. What could he possibly want with her? Nothing good, she was pretty sure. He probably wanted to bawl her out for being ungracious to Belinda yesterday. She didn't doubt that the other woman had told him about the scene in the supermarket.

"Wh-what does he want?" she stammered.

"He wants to talk to you," Amber said reasonably.

Kirsten glanced at Coralie and saw that she was glowing with excitement. "For heaven's sake don't sit there like a ninny," her friend prodded. "Go talk to him. Take it upstairs, where you'll have some privacy. Now hurry!"

Kirsten bounded off the couch and rushed up the stairs, more in reaction to Coralie's urgency than her own. She didn't want to listen to Sam berate her. Why didn't he just leave her alone? All she wanted was to get away from him and his ex-fiancée before the situation got any more agonizing.

She'd slowed down by the time she got to the top of the stairs, but nevertheless she was wheezing. She coughed and took a deep breath as she walked into the master bedroom and headed for the phone on the desk. The last thing she needed was for Sam to hear her raspy breathing.

She picked up the receiver and only then realized she was shaking. Not only her hands but all over.

"H-hello," she said barely above a whisper.

"Kirsten? This is Sam," he said, as if she wouldn't know his voice anywhere. "What's the matter? I can hardly hear you."

She took another deep breath. "N-nothing," she replied and this time it came out clearer and more forceful. "I'm just a little out of breath from running up the stairs. Coralie suggested I take the call up here where...where it's not so noisy," she finished, not exactly truthfully.

There was a long moment of silence when each apparently waited for the other to speak. Finally Sam broke it. "I wanted to let you know I'll pick you up at about six tomorrow night, if that time is okay with you."

Kirsten blinked and tossed her head. Was there something wrong with her ears as well as her breathing? He couldn't possibly have said what she thought he did.

"Pick me up tomorrow?" Damn, she sounded like an idiot.

There was a second's hesitation. "Yes. To take you t

the potluck supper and dance. You do remember agreeing to go with me, don't you?'' He sounded impatient and a little sarcastic.

The monthly potluck supper and dance at the lodge hall. He'd asked her to go with him at Jim's birthday party! In all the upheaval since then she'd forgotten all about it, but even if she'd remembered she would have assumed that he didn't still intend to take her. That scene on Tuesday had been pretty final.

She put her hand over the mouthpiece as another wheeze rattled her chest. She was going to have to wind this up quickly.

"Actually, I had forgotten," she admitted, "but even if I'd remembered I wouldn't have expected you... I mean you were pretty mad at me, and now that Belinda's back I would have thought you'd take her.''

Again she put her hand over the mouthpiece to cover up the sound of another wheeze.

"I didn't ask Belinda, I asked you.'' Now he sounded angry. "Do you want to go or not?''

Kirsten winced. Romeo he wasn't. "Not if you feel you have to take me,'' she said tightly. "I'm sure I can find another date if I decide to attend.''

She wished she could take back the words the minute they were out. There was no excuse for her being nasty to him.

"Fine,'' he said and hung up.

She sat for a while just looking at the telephone, then put it back in its cradle. *Fool!* she chastised herself. *Now he's sure you're a tart, and you have nobody to blame but yourself. Doesn't it ever occur to you to hold your tongue? You could have been gracious, even though he wasn't.*

There was a lump in her throat, a clatter in her chest and tears in her eyes. She wished she'd never come to Copper Canyon, Idaho! She'd been doing just fine without a special man in her life until she met up with Sam Lawford. She hadn't even wanted one. She could always get an escort when she needed one, and she'd enjoyed her freedom.

If only Coralie hadn't answered that ad for a mail-order wife and come here to meet Jim. If only she hadn't also met Dr. Sam and decided he was just the man for Kirsten. If only Kirsten had resisted her pleas to come for a visit...

If only. If only. If only. She stifled a sob, and realized she was panting. Not a good sign. She needed another treatment with the bronchial dilator, but she would have to go downstairs to get it, along with the medicine in her purse.

She stood and walked to the top of the stairs, but by the time she got there she felt dizzy and sank down on the top step. There was no hiding it now, she would have to ask Coralie for help.

"Coralie," she called. "My purse is on the floor by the couch in the living room. Would you bring it to me please?"

"Sure," Coralie answered in a puzzled tone. "Just a second."

Kirsten heard her walking around, and then she appeared in the front hallway. She looked up and saw Kirsten sitting on the top stair. "Is everything okay?" she asked as she started up the stairs, then paused when Kirsten started to cough and wheeze.

"Oh jeez, it's another asthma attack," she said anxiously as she hurried to Kirsten. "Did you tell Sam? I'll drive you to the hospital...."

"No!" Kirsten commanded as she struggled to suppress another coughing spell. "I'll be all right...just need a treatment with the dilator...in my purse."

Coralie didn't argue, but helped Kirsten to stand and led her into the master bathroom.

Half an hour later Kirsten had stopped wheezing and her cough was much better. She sat on the edge of the bathtub while Coralie cleaned and repackaged her medical paraphernalia.

"This isn't the first time this has happened since you've been here, is it?" she asked accusingly. "Why didn't you tell me, Kirsten? You know better than to mess around with this stuff."

Kirsten felt drained. "I've been using the dilator for a couple of days, but this is the first time the attack has been this bad."

"What did Sam say?" Coralie asked. "Is he coming out or does he want you to go to the hospital?"

Kirsten shook her head. "I didn't tell him about it."

Coralie looked stricken. "Whyever not? Good God, girl, you need oxygen and the breathing machine."

"No, really, I'm breathing just fine now," Kirsten insisted. "I don't want Sam to know about this. Please promise me you won't tell him. I'll see my own doctor just as soon as I get back to Eureka."

"You're not going to try to drive all the way to California in your condition!" Coralie exclaimed.

Kirsten smiled. "My condition's just fine, as long as I don't get too upset. Sam and I had an argument on the phone, and I guess that's what brought this one on."

She saw the anger building in Coralie and hastened to assure her. "It's not his fault. He doesn't know, and you're not going to tell him. Promise me," she demanded again.

The phone rang, but someone answered it downstairs.

"I'm not going to promise anything until I see where this is going," Coralie grumbled. "I'll abide by your wishes for now, but I'm going to keep a close eye on you and if I see any signs of respiratory distress I'm going to take you to the hospital if I have to tie you down to get you in the car."

"Kirsten," Amber shouted up the stairs. "Telephone for you."

Kirsten stood up, still feeling a little shaky. "That's probably Butch at the garage. He said he'd call when the computer for the car came in."

They walked out of the bathroom into the bedroom, then Kirsten headed for the phone while Coralie went back downstairs.

Kirsten picked it up and said hello.

"Kirsten, this is Sam. Please don't hang up. I want to apologize."

Chapter Ten

There was a pleading tone in Sam's voice that went straight to Kirsten's heart. She couldn't have cut him off even if she'd wanted to, and she definitely didn't want to.

"I'm not going to hang up," she said shakily. "Actually I'm the one who should apologize. I didn't mean to be so sharp with you, it's just that you took me by surprise. After the way I behaved the last time we talked, I really didn't expect to see or hear from you again."

She heard him clear his throat. "I guess we were both pretty much off base that day. I'll have to admit I was awfully upset and started making accusations and demands that I had no right to make—"

"Sam, you had every right to be upset and angry with me. I'm sorry you were so worried when you didn't know where I was, but that's not what I'm talking about—"

"I know what you're getting at, Kirsten," he said gently, "and your relationship with other men is none of my business. I'm the one who set the limits for you and me. You don't owe me anything. If you no longer want to go with me tomorrow night I'll understand, but my invitation stands. I'd like very much to take you to the supper and dance. It's not an obligation, it will be my pleasure.''

Tears gathered behind her eyes and formed a lump in her throat as she swallowed back a sob. "I'd love to go with you, Sam.'' Her voice was little more than a whisper. "Six o'clock will be fine. What food would you like me to bring?''

Again he cleared his throat, and she wondered if he was as emotionally precarious as she. "That won't be necessary,'' he told her. "My housekeeper is going to fix a casserole for us to take.''

Kirsten managed a breathless little laugh. "That's good, because cooking is not one of the things I excel at.''

He chuckled, then sobered. "Don't apologize. I can always hire a cook, but you have a warm, caring nature and that can't be bought. I'll pick you up tomorrow evening at the big house. Until then, goodbye.''

He broke the connection, and left Kirsten with tears of both joy and regret spilling down her cheeks.

The following day Kirsten and Coralie went shopping along Copper Canyon's five-block Main Street in search of something informal but dressy to wear that night. Coralie, Jim and the girls were going, too, and both Coralie and Jim were elated that Sam was taking Kirsten.

After searching through the women's wear section of both small department stores, one a chain and the other locally owned, and finding nothing that excited them, they discovered Yvonne's Boutique. It was a small but classy women's dress shop situated on a side street in the first floor of a big old two-story house.

The owner, a strikingly pretty redheaded woman in her early thirties, introduced herself as Yvonne Stuart, wife of one of the town's lawyers. She understood exactly what they were looking for, and within an hour had outfitted them both. Kirsten with a three-tiered blue chambray skirt and a matching vest that would be worn with a white blouse she already owned, and Coralie with a sheer rose-print broomstick skirt and a deeper plain rose knit tunic. A narrow silver metal belt completed the ensemble.

"You two ladies will be the belles of the ball," Yvonne said as she handed them their packages. "I understand they have live music for tonight. Billy Gene Wyatt and His Rhythm Makers. From what I hear just about everybody in town will be there."

They thanked her and turned to leave, when the door opened and Belinda stepped inside. As usual she was fastidiously dressed and made up, but for the first few seconds her expression was somber, almost glum. Then she looked up and saw Kirsten and Coralie and smiled pleasantly although her eyes were cold.

"Well for goodness' sake you two do get around," she said breezily. "You seem to pop up every place I go."

That thought had occurred to Kirsten, too. Was it really coincidence or was Belinda keeping track of her? She banished the thought and chided herself for getting paranoid.

"We needed something to wear to the dance tonight," Coralie said politely but with a not quite concealed note of irritation in her tone. "We'll no doubt run into you again there."

Belinda's smile vanished. "Oh, no, I'm afraid not. Sam asked me to go with him, but I'd already accepted an invitation to have dinner with friends in Grangeville. He was disappointed, but..."

She continued talking, but Kirsten lost track of what was being said as she struggled to hide her shock and anger. Was she telling the truth? Had Sam only asked Kirsten to go with him after he'd been turned down by Belinda?

A searing pain swept through her, but she wasn't going to let the other woman see it. Sam had always struck her as an honest man and he'd told her that he hadn't invited Belinda to the dance. But how could she be sure he wasn't just feeding her a line when he found himself without a date and belatedly remembered that he'd asked her earlier?

Finally she managed to gain control of her voice and interrupted the conversation. "Coralie, we really must get started back to the farm."

Coralie looked a little startled, but she immediately got the message. "You're right," she said, looking at her watch. "Goodbye, Belinda. Have a nice time at your dinner party."

On the way home Kirsten was stony faced and silent, so Coralie got the conversation started. "Don't pay attention to anything that woman says. She's lying through her teeth about Sam asking her first."

"How can you be sure?" Kirsten replied grumpily. "You don't know her any better than I do."

"No, I don't," her friend agreed, "but I've gotten to know Sam very well during the short time I've been here. Remember, he and Jim are best friends, and they are always relaxed and off guard with each other.

"Sam wouldn't lie to you. He wouldn't even stretch the truth. If he hadn't wanted to take you out, he wouldn't have called and asked you to go. He's a bright guy. He knew he was off the hook after that big blowup you two had. If he wanted a date, you're the last person he'd have been obliged to call after you implied that you'd spent the night making love with Don."

"That's right," Kirsten agreed. "So why did he call me? I still can't figure that out."

"He called because he wanted you to go with him," Coralie explained patiently. "Apparently he managed to convince you of that yesterday or you wouldn't have agreed to it. Don't let that witch throw you. She's just mad because he's not taking her."

What Coralie said made sense, and Kirsten felt a little better, but her joy had been dimmed and her eagerness subdued.

* * *

Later that afternoon Kirsten spent considerable time getting ready for her date with Sam, and when she finished she had to admit that the Western look suited her. At midcalf length, the skirt was longer than she usually wore but it was full and swirled gracefully around her legs when she moved. The matching vest was trimmed with fringe along the bottom.

She made sure to be at the big house by five-thirty, in case Sam arrived early. She wanted lots of people around when they first met again. Being alone with him at the cottage would be too awkward. They needed someone else to break the ice.

Kirsten was upstairs in Gloria's room at six o'clock helping the girl plait her luxurious dark brown hair into a french braid when the doorbell rang. Her stomach muscles clenched and her heartbeat sped up as she forced herself to stand still and continue what she was doing. There were plenty of other people to answer the door.

In a matter of seconds she heard Coralie and Sam greeting each other, then Jim's voice was added. Gloria caught Kirsten's glance in the mirror of the vanity. "There's Dr. Sam," she said excitedly. "You go on down. I can manage okay."

"Are you sure?" Kirsten asked, wishing for an excuse to hide.

Just then Coralie called up the stairs, "Kirsten, Sam's here." And that tenuous hope vanished.

"Be right down," she called back, then anchored the braid she was working on before she turned and headed for the stairway.

Sam was standing directly below her and looked up when he heard her footsteps on the hardwood floor. Admiration shone in his expressive brown eyes, and she caught her breath and reached for the railing before she started down.

Damn, why did he have to be so...so *sexy* looking? He was wearing brown Western-style pants and a fitted cream shirt with pearl snap buttons and a turquoise bolo. He would never be mistaken for a rugged cowboy, but he sure looked like the stylized version of one in *GQ*.

She had to clutch the rail to keep from running down the stairs and throwing herself at him. From the way he was looking at her she dared to hope that he might even welcome such a greeting.

She noticed that he also had one hand on the railing. "Hello, Kirsten." His tone was low and husky. "You look especially beautiful."

She wasn't sure how to respond. He was probably just saying that to be polite. "Hello, Sam," she replied shyly, feeling like a schoolgirl on her first date. "You look nice, too."

Jim and Coralie were standing beside them, and Jim chuckled. "I suspect we're going to have far and away the prettiest girls there," he observed to Sam.

"Women!" Coralie and Kirsten chorused in unison, and Sam and Jim broke into laughter.

"Yes ma'am," Jim said empathetically and put his arm around his wife. "Women it is, even though mine isn't much older than my eldest daughter."

"Now you stop that," Coralie said firmly even as she snuggled into his embrace. "I'm plenty old enough to be your wife."

"Oh yes, my darling, you surely are," he said with obviously more of a sensual undertone than he'd intended.

Coralie blushed and buried her face in his shoulder, and he looked a little sheepish. "Sorry, guys," he said to Kirsten and Sam, "but as you may have guessed, I adore my young bride."

Kirsten felt herself tearing up again. "That's nothing to apologize for," she said through trembling lips. "All of us *girls* should be as lucky as Coralie."

She'd accented the word *girls* to keep a light tone, but she was deadly serious. She would sell her soul for a man who would love her the way Jim loved Coralie.

Sam hadn't missed any of the implications of this little byplay, either. He'd recognized almost from the beginning that Kirsten wasn't as sophisticated as she would like people to think. She would never be a dedicated career woman. By her own admission she wanted a home with a husband and assorted children. She would never give up nursing altogether, but her family would always come first with her.

That was the reason he'd warned her from the start about his intentions. Why he'd made it plain that marriage wasn't for him.

So what in hell went wrong? Why was he trying so hard to repair the latest rupture in their relationship? Why couldn't he leave her alone? She would be going back to California very shortly and then he would never see her again, so why hadn't he just left things the way they were?

Was it possible that he was trying to get back at her for sleeping with Don Sterling? That had been a blow that nearly shattered him, but there was no reason for him to react the way he had. He had no hold on her. In fact he'd gone to great pains to make sure she understood that. There was no future for them together, and therefore they were both free to sleep with whomever they wanted.

Like hell! The very thought of her cuddling up with Sterling was like a stab in the heart.

Sam was jerked out of his musing by the sound of a door slamming on the second floor and Jim's two teenage daughters yelling at each other as they came down the stairs.

"Did not!" Gloria said.

"Did too!" insisted Amber.

"Did not!"

"Did too!"

"Hey, you two!" Jim yelled. "Knock it off. What's the problem?"

Sam figured this was no place for outsiders and he touched Kirsten's arm. "I think we'd better go, okay?"

"By all means," she said as she let him lead her outside, down the steps and help her into the car.

On the way into town they sat side by side in strained silence. Sam seemed preoccupied, and Kirsten was still wrestling with the suspicion that she was his second choice after being turned down by his precious Belinda. She was tempted to ask him, but didn't want to start another quarrel and ruin the evening altogether.

"Your housekeeper's casserole smells delicious," she said instead, as she identified the aroma of chicken, broccoli and mushroom soup coming from the back of the car. It made her mouth water.

"Yes, Esther's an excellent cook," he agreed somewhat stiffly. "She comes in to clean and cook for me on Monday, Wednesday and Friday. She made the casserole yesterday, so all I had to do was put it in the oven and heat it up."

Once they'd exhausted that topic, the uneasy quiet resumed. The subjects of Belinda and Don that screamed to be explored were taboo, and nothing else seemed important enough to talk about.

"Are you... That is, have you been having a good visit with Jim and Coralie?" he stammered.

They were one subject Kirsten was happy to discuss. "Oh yes, it's been wonderful. Jim is a great guy and Coralie's so happy. I understand there was something of a problem with his daughters for a while, but if so it's all been ironed out."

She sighed. "I encouraged Coralie to answer that ad for a mail-order wife, so I'm especially relieved that it turned out so well. I'd have felt responsible if it hadn't."

Sam looked at her and frowned. "That's a dangerous thing to do. The man placing the ad could have been mentally deranged. I hope you aren't going to try the same thing."

Kirsten winced, but the blow struck anyway. Damn him! She should have expected it. He never missed a chance to let her know he still thought she was too irresponsible to make intelligent decisions. He'd been mad at her from the moment they met, and that anger was never far from the surface no matter how much he tried to deny it.

"Sam," she said icily, "I'm getting awfully tired of being your punching bag."

His eyes widened with a look of disbelief. "Punching bag!" he exploded. "I've never laid a hand on you with anything but tenderness!"

"Not physically, no," she admitted, "but verbal abuse is just as painful."

The blood drained from his face. "Verbal abuse! Kirsten, I realize I was pretty hard on you when you ran into my car, but I swear to God I've never intentionally hurt you, verbally or otherwise. Will you please tell me what you're talking about?"

Kirsten wasn't buying that line. "You just can't resist throwing that up to me. You never miss a chance to point out how stupid, immature and...and *unworthy* I am—"

"*Unworthy!*" Sam howled. "What in hell does that mean?"

"It means unable to measure up," she snapped waspishly. "Like in, I'm not worthy to take Belinda's place in your life, but I'm okay as a fill-in when she's occupied elsewhere—"

Sam swore lustily. "How did Belinda get into this conversation? Damn it, Kirsten, I don't have the vaguest idea what happened to set you off this way. Have you been talking to Belinda? Did she do or say something to upset you...?"

His words finally cut through the haze of her anger and registered. She could see by his expression and his body language that he truly didn't have any idea what she was talking about. But how was that possible? Unless...unless Belinda really had deliberately lied earlier that day.

Suddenly the powerful engine revved up and the car roared past the street where they should have turned, startling her. "Sam! Where are you going?"

He looked straight ahead. "I'm taking you to my house," he said grimly. "We're going to get this mess straightened out now."

Before she could protest he made a sharp turn left, then right, then left again while she hung on to the armrest to keep from being bounced around. Finally he slowed down and made a last left turn, this time into the driveway of his impressive home.

Kirsten still gripped the armrest when Sam got out of the car and came around to open her door. "I'm sorry if I scared you." He reached in to help her out. "Come on. We'll go inside and have a drink and then we'll have a long overdue chat."

Her knees shook as she climbed out of the car and followed Sam to his front door. Not from the wild ride, but from the onslaught of emotions that had been buffeting her all day.

Maybe she should just ditch her car here and take the first flight back to California. Jim wouldn't mind selling it for her, and if she didn't get out of here she was sure to have either another asthma attack or an emotional breakdown.

Inside Sam seated her in the living room in a big, comfortable overstuffed chair and excused himself. He was back in a few minutes with two brandy snifters and handed one to her. "Here, sip it even if you don't particularly like it. It will help calm us both down."

She tasted the amber liquor and wrinkled her nose as Sam took a seat on the sofa. "Yuck," she said inelegantly.

Sam chuckled and took a swig of his. "It'll burn a little as it goes down, but it's good at calming nerves."

She leaned back in the chair and sipped slowly. If taken in very small doses she noted that it went down more easily and did help to relax her.

Glancing over at Sam she saw that he was sitting forward with his arms resting on his thighs and twirling the brandy in his glass. He looked perturbed, and she had the dreaded feeling that she'd overreacted again.

She took another sip. Darn. What had gotten into her lately? Usually she was mild tempered even when she had good and compelling reason not to be. But she and Sam just seemed to rub each other the wrong way.

She shivered and closed her eyes. On second thought he could rub her any way he wanted to and the sooner the better. She could almost feel his strong, smooth hands massaging her bare flesh. They would be warm and his fingers would know just where to touch and knead and slide—

"Kirsten." His voice broke into her steamy thoughts and nearly made her spill her drink. "Tell me why you're so upset with me. Even if you think I already know, or at least should know, tell me anyway because I haven't a clue and it's not fair to either of us to make me guess."

"No, you're right, it isn't," she acknowledged. "Just answer one question for me."

"Of course I will." His tone was low and intense. "I haven't any secrets from you. What do you want to know?"

Kirsten sighed. It was now or never. If she didn't ask the questions, she would never slake her burning need to know.

She looked down and away from him when she spoke. "Sam, did you ask Belinda Evans to go with you to the dance tonight before you asked me?"

He uttered a sort of choking sound, but she still didn't look up. "What kind of a question is that? Belinda wasn't even in town when I asked you. If you remember, she didn't show up until the following evening."

Kirsten shook her head. "No, that's not what I mean. After that quarrel we had on Tuesday when I got back from the mountains, I can't believe that you weren't washing your hands of me when you shot out of the driveway and headed back into town. For days after that I didn't hear anything from you, and I was too upset to even remember we had a date for tonight until you called and reminded me. Then this morning Coralie and I were in town doing some shopping and we ran into Belinda. She told us you'd asked her to go with you tonight but she had to turn you down because she had a previous engagement.''

This time he did choke, and Kirsten looked up. He was staring at her wide-eyed with disbelief. ''Belinda told you that? But that's nonsense. I admit I was damn mad at you, but my better sense gradually took over and I cooled down. I never even talked to Belinda about the dance tonight. You just misunderstood her.''

Kirsten was incensed. *Oh sure, blame me. It's all my fault. Ex-lover Belinda would never lie or cheat or twist the truth. Therefore I'm the troublemaker. The one who's too stupid to decipher a simple conversation.*

She clamped her jaws together and counted to ten. She wasn't going to let the thought of that woman goad her into losing her temper and behaving like a spoiled child again. It was time she grew up and started acting like a rational adult.

''No, Sam,'' she said coolly. ''I didn't misunderstand. Coralie was with me. She'll tell you exactly what was said. My problem is that I don't like being a substitute for another woman, and that's what I've been with you all along.''

He closed his eyes and shook his head. ''No, that's not true. I hadn't seen or talked to Belinda in eight years, until this week—''

''I know that,'' Kirsten said sadly, ''but she's been the most important woman in your life all this time. You even admitted it. You told me you'd never marry or become deeply involved with a woman again because of the way she'd betrayed you. An attitude like that gives her an awful lot of power over you. You've been letting her jerk you around all these years whether you recognize it or not, and now she's come back to continue doing it in person.''

She put her glass on the table and stood. ''I suppose you can't help it. Love isn't always rational, and a good lot of the time it's blind. Take it from me, I know, but I'm not going to stay around and try to save you from her smothering influence.''

He winced and his expression turned icy as he stood up, too. ''You don't think much of me, do you.'' It was a statement, not a question.

She felt as if her heart was being chipped into little chunks. ''I wish that were true,'' she said mournfully, ''but unfortunately I don't have any more control over who I fall in love with than you do. I care very much for you, but I intend to fight it. I'm going to live my life to the fullest, and not just exist because I fell in lust with the wrong man!''

Sam blinked. ''Are you admitting that what you feel for me is lust and not love?''

That brought her up short. ''I don't know,'' she said thoughtfully. ''I have trouble separating the two emotions in my mind. I can't imagine being intimate with a man I don't love, or at least think I do.''

Sam looked surprised. ''Then what about Don Sterling? Did you think you were in love with him last Monday when you spent the night with him? If so, your feelings for me can't be very deep.''

She was caught totally off guard. Darn! She kept getting bogged down in her own evasions. Now she would have to tell Sam the truth about that night.

She picked up her glass and took a sip of the brandy, then cupped it in her hands as she walked over to the big old-fashioned window and stood with her back to him.

"You probably won't believe this," she said haltingly, "but Don and I didn't make love that night."

She paused expecting a reaction, but there was none so she continued. "I...I didn't exactly lie to you, I just sort of let you draw your own conclusions."

Again she paused, but there was still no reaction from Sam, which surprised and flustered her. "I did spend the night at the cabin with him, but I slept in the bedroom and he made himself a bed on the couch. He...he was a gentleman and a friend all the time I was there. He didn't even make a pass at me or say anything suggestive. It...it was grossly unfair, both to him and to you, for me to let you think he had."

Still Sam didn't move or speak, and Kirsten couldn't stand the throbbing suspense of silence a minute longer.

She tossed back a swallow of her brandy and turned to face him. He was just standing there looking at her, and it unnerved her more than if he'd ranted and raged. "Sam? Aren't you going to say something?" It sounded like a plea, and of course it was.

His expression didn't alter. "What do you want me to say?" His tone was cool and deliberate.

"I...I don't know. Just say something. I know that what I did was unforgivable, and I'm truly sorry—"

"Then why did you do it?" His tone was disapproving.

"I was hurt and angry with you over the way you'd practically ignored me the night before when Belinda reentered your life. I'd gone to your house expecting to...that is..."

"Expecting to make love?" he said softly. "I was expecting that, too. I'd looked forward to it ever since I left you at your door the night before, but when Belinda showed up so unexpectedly... Well, the shock really threw me. If you'd just stayed with me a little longer I would have sent her away. I *did* send her away, but by the time I'd collected my wits enough to do so you were gone, too."

Kirsten was stunned. "But why? You said you were in love with her!"

Sam moved then and walked over to stand beside her. "Apparently you misunderstood what I told you about Belinda," he said bluntly. "It's true, I was deeply, passionately in love with her at the time she left, and the pain I felt when she deserted me for another man was excruciating, but I got over that."

Kirsten caught her breath as Sam continued. "I didn't mean to imply that I've been carrying a torch for her all these years, waiting and hoping she'd come back to me. We'd known each other all our lives and I'd trusted her completely. It's the broken trust I can't forget. If Belinda could do something like that to me after all we'd been to each other, how can I ever have faith in another woman not to do the same thing?"

He reached out and pulled the lace curtains apart so that the view of the snow-covered mountains in the distance was unobstructed. "I don't want her now. Even if I still loved her, I could never rely on her again. She's the last person I'd take back into my life. The only contact I've had with her since she came here again is when she's gotten in touch with me. If she's told you otherwise she's lying, and I'll certainly have words with her about it."

Kirsten felt as if a weight had been lifted from her. It was obvious that Sam wasn't about to get involved with Belinda again. He was no longer deceived by her pretty face and seductive ways.

On the other hand it didn't change a thing in his relationship with Kirsten, either, and her relief dimmed. It only strengthened his determination to never trust another woman with his happiness.

She took a deep breath and pasted a big smile on her face. "Well, now that we've got that straightened out I think we'd better go over to the lodge hall before the food's all gone. I don't want to miss out on all that good home cooking.''

Sam glanced at his watch. "You're right. Of course we've always got Esther's casserole to munch on if that happens.''

The lodge hall was big with a stage at one end that had been set up with chairs and music stands for the musicians, who hadn't started playing yet. There were long fold-up tables with benches strategically placed on the floor, and the buffet tables along one wall held plenty of food for the latecomers who were still arriving.

Sam and Kirsten were greeted enthusiastically by everyone they bumped into. They finally made their way to the food and filled their plates, then took them to the table where Jim and Coralie were just finishing up their supper.

"Hey, we'd about given up on you two," Jim said jovially as the couple sat down across from them.

"Sorry," Sam said, though he didn't look it. "We stopped by the house for a drink. Did we miss anything?"

"I doubt it," Jim said slyly, "but if you did you can always catch up later.''

Kirsten blushed at the double entendre, even as a grin twitched her mouth. "Where are the girls?" she asked Coralie.

Coralie shrugged. "Who knows. They bolted through their food and took off with a group of friends. They're around here someplace.''

By the time Kirsten and Sam finished eating, the kitchen crew was folding up the empty tables and putting them away. A short time later the six-piece orchestra assembled on the stage and started playing.

The first set was two mixers where the dancers changed partners every few minutes. It was frustrating for Kirsten because Sam would no sooner get his arm around her than she was twirled away to another man. One of them was

Don Sterling, and seeing him reminded her that Sam hadn't said whether or not he believed her when she told him that she and Don hadn't slept together.

The second set was line dances, where they all danced in a row instead of together, so it wasn't until the third set that they danced together the good old-fashioned way.

The music was golden oldies from the big-band era, slow and rhythmic and romantic. "Let Me Call You Sweetheart," "When I Waltz Again With You" and "Mockingbird Hill." Sam held out his arms and she melted into them as they moved gracefully across the floor. He put both arms around her waist, and she twined hers around his neck as they swayed in time to the music. "Thank God those clowns finally slowed down and started playing music that gives me an excuse to hold you," he murmured in her ear.

She snuggled closer. "Do you need an excuse?" Her voice was low and seductive.

"Not unless you do." His arms tightened around her with one hand on the rise of her buttocks and the other in the middle of her back so that their bodies were pressed together as one.

Fortunately the lights on the dance floor were dimmed, and to any onlookers the dancers were shadowy couples weaving in, out and around one another though not clearly defined.

Sam and Kirsten continued to hold each other between songs as they waited on the floor for the next one, standing silently, not daring to speak for fear of breaking the spell that held them enthralled.

Chapter Eleven

The hours passed in a romantic haze as Kirsten and Sam danced, then held hands and visited with friends between sets. To Kirsten's mind what had started as an "iffy" date evolved into a magical experience rivaling Cinderella's ball.

She and Sam had finally straightened out their misunderstandings and were no longer fighting their feelings for each other. She had openly declared her love for him, and while he hadn't told her he loved her he let his actions speak for him. He was warm and caring and couldn't keep his hands off her.

They were building up to the climax of making love. She couldn't be mistaken about that. Each time he took her in his arms and moved so seductively with her to the beat of the music, the rhythm of love, was a restrained act of foreplay. As the evening wore on she kept expecting him to suggest they leave early, but apparently he preferred to savor the excitement and suspense as long as possible.

Which was fine with her. It proved that he didn't just want sexual release, he wanted to make love with her in every sense of the word. That just made the anticipation all the sweeter.

At midnight the orchestra played the last waltz, another oldie titled "Goodnight, Sweetheart," that left Kirsten aglow with romantic fantasies as she and Sam held each other close and undulated to the soft strains of the melody. When it was over they refused all invitations to go to private homes for more dessert and coffee, said their goodnights and hurried to the car.

Kirsten had expected Sam to take her to his house, but instead he turned in the opposite direction and headed toward the farm. She was a little surprised, but it didn't matter to her where they went as long as they spent the rest of the night together.

When they pulled into the driveway the big house was dark except for the porch light, which indicated that the Buckleys weren't home yet. Kirsten's porch light at the cottage was on, too, and Sam parked the car in front and shut off the motor. But instead of opening his door he turned in his seat and reached for her.

"I've been aching to kiss you all night," he said huskily, "and I can't wait a second longer."

He lowered his head and covered her mouth with his. Her soft gasp relaxed her lips and he parted them with the tip of his tongue and took possession.

Kirsten's heart hammered as he cupped her breast and gently caressed it with his fingers. In her excitement she bit his lower lip gently. He retaliated by sucking on her tongue and sending tremors to the pit of her stomach and beyond.

She shivered, and in her eagerness to pleasure him as he was pleasuring her she put her hand on his hip and kneaded it through his trousers.

"Oh, that feels so good," he said shakily as he grasped her skirt and slowly bunched it up until he could put his hand on her bare thigh.

Before she could catch her breath he began stroking her thigh. The ecstasy of his touch was so sharp that she cried out, but he misunderstood and immediately removed his hand.

"I'm sorry," he said anxiously. "Did I offend you?"

Offend her! How could such a tender and intimate caress be offensive? Kirsten was thoroughly frustrated. "No," she gasped as she rubbed her face in his chest. "Oh no, please don't stop."

She picked up his hand and put it back where it had been, but just then a loud *beep! beep! beep!* startled her so that she jumped away from him.

"Son of a....!" Sam bit back the oath and reached in his pocket. "It's only my beeper, sweetheart," he explained and shut it off as he turned on the dome light so he could look at it. "Damn! It's the hospital. May I use your phone?"

Kirsten nodded, still too disconcerted to speak, and they got out of the car and hurried into the house.

She took him to the phone in the bedroom, then went into the living room to give him some privacy. He joined her almost immediately, looking distraught. "There's an emergency patient at the hospital. Sorry, but I have to leave immediately."

Her dream of a night of bliss evaporated, but she knew he was as frustrated as she. "Of course," she said. "Can I be of any help? I'd be more than willing to go with you—"

"No!" It was a short but emphatic statement. "That... that won't be necessary. There's an RN on duty."

A feeling of dread rolled through Kirsten. What was wrong? Doctors didn't get as upset as Sam obviously was over an emergency illness or accident unless the patient was somebody dear to them—

"Sam, who's the patient?" Her anxiety rose. "Dear Lord, it's not Coralie or Jim—"

He reached out and took her by the upper arms. "No, Kirsten, it's not either of them."

"Then who? Is it Amber or Gloria?" She was well aware that doctors didn't usually give out information about their patients, but this was different. He was too shaken. His face was white, and he was anything but dispassionate. This patient was someone special to him.

"No, it isn't any of the Buckley family. It...it's Belinda. Her mother found her lying across her bed unconscious. Now I really must go. I'll call you." He turned and rushed out of the house leaving Kirsten stunned and alone.

Kirsten got little rest that night. Mostly she tossed and turned, while questions with no answers beleaguered her.

What was wrong with Belinda? Was she sick? She'd certainly seemed well enough that morning at the boutique. Was she injured? If Sam knew, he hadn't mentioned it. Had it been a heart attack? A stroke? But she was too young for either of those ailments.

Why was Sam so upset about her health when he'd just told Kirsten that evening that he was no longer in love with Belinda and didn't want to marry her? That was the question that tormented her.

Not that she thought he'd been lying to her, but was it possible that he was lying to himself? Did he deny his deep feelings for her, even to himself, because he knew she couldn't be trusted? Or because he suspected that she wasn't capable of loving anybody but herself?

There were so many reasons for him not to get involved with Belinda again, but there were people as well as animals who mated for life and were never able to form a lasting bond with anyone else. Was Sam one of them? Kirsten strongly suspected he was, and that meant she didn't stand an ice cube's chance in hell with him. Her only hope for marriage and a family was to get as far away from him as she could and as soon as possible.

She was up before sunrise the next morning, and when she was sure Jim would be out of the big house she walked over to see Coralie. The gossip had already started, and apparently phones had been ringing all over the area with the news.

"Jim and I heard it even before we got home from the dance last night," Coralie told her. "We'd been invited along with several other couples to Dave and Sally Roberts's house for dessert and coffee. He's publisher of the local newspaper, you know, and one of his reporters called it in from the hospital. All the reporter knew was that Belinda had been rushed there by ambulance, but the hospital wasn't giving out any information."

Kirsten already knew that. "How is she? Have you heard anything new this morning? Does anybody know what happened?"

Coralie sighed. "There are a lot of rumors, but none that I'd take seriously. Jim will get in touch with her parents when he comes in for dinner. He knows them well. He and Sam practically grew up at the Evans' house, since their parents were all close friends and the kids were all the same age. Until then, I don't want to speculate."

Kirsten wondered what it was she didn't want to speculate about, but refrained from asking. Coralie would tell her as soon as she was reasonably sure she had the right story.

Kirsten didn't hear from Sam that morning, but when Jim came in at noon he did call Mrs. Evans. When he hung up, he turned to Coralie, Kirsten and his two daughters who were old enough to pick up on what was going on in the town.

"Maybelle says that Belinda was feeling depressed last night, so she took some sleeping pills and went to bed early. She went to sleep but woke up a little while later, thought she'd been asleep longer than she had and took more pills. When Maybelle looked in on her before going to bed her-

elf, she found Belinda unconscious and called the ambu-
ance.''

"She took an overdose of sleeping pills?" Coralie and
Kirsten gasped at the same time, then remembered there
were teenagers present and snapped their mouths shut.

Jim nodded. "She's apparently been pretty upset about
he problems with her husband and all the ramifications of
he divorce and hasn't been able to sleep. They pumped
er stomach and she's okay. She'll be going home later this
fternoon.''

Coralie and Kirsten looked at each other but didn't com-
nent.

Sam didn't get in touch with Kirsten until later that af-
ernoon when he caught up with her by phone at the cot-
age. "Sorry I didn't get back to you sooner," he said,
ounding more like a wary physician than a potential lover.
'It was too late to call when I left the hospital last night,
nd you may remember that I temporarily have office hours
n Sunday mornings.''

Kirsten had forgotten it was Sunday. "How is Belinda?''
he asked.

"She'll be all right. She's out of the hospital now and
ack home with her parents.''

Kirsten hesitated then plunged ahead. "I understand she
ook an overdose of sleeping pills?''

His answer was short and sharp. "Yes.''

She knew she should leave it alone but she couldn't.
Was it accidental or deliberate?''

He sighed. "You know I can't discuss that with you over
ie telephone. I need to see you. Will you have dinner with
ie tonight? There's a new restaurant in Grangeville that I
nderstand serves good food.''

She didn't know whether to be thrilled or apprehensive.
e sounded as if the need to see her was more of a duty
ian a pleasure. Plus, why would he want to take her to a

restaurant more than ten miles away when there were perfectly good ones in Copper Canyon?

"I'd love to have dinner with you," she answered, and it was the truth. No matter what his purpose in taking her out, she couldn't control her eager anticipation.

"Good. I'll pick you up at the big house at six. Bye." He broke the connection, leaving her more puzzled and disappointed than before. They wouldn't have any privacy at all if she met him at Jim and Coralie's. Had he planned it that way? But why?

Kirsten had been ready and waiting at the big house with the Buckley family for more than half an hour by the time Sam arrived. She'd chosen to wear leggings and a rib-textured cotton knit pullover tunic dyed to match in a dusty teal color. An outfit that was both casual and understatedly sexy.

She heard his car turn into the driveway, but forced herself to wait until the bell rang before answering it. Something wasn't quite right, and she wanted to know what was going on before she made a public spectacle of herself by falling all over him.

Coralie and Gloria were putting the finishing touches on supper, Jim was washing up and Amber was setting the table. Kirsten hoped, since there was no one in the vicinity of the doorway, that Sam would take her in his arms and maybe even give her a kiss, but it didn't happen.

Instead, he looked grim as he pulled open the screen door and stepped inside. "You're all ready, I see." His gaze softened as his eyes roamed over her. "And beautiful as ever."

"Thank you. It's sweet of you to say so," she answered, and stood aside to let him enter. She hoped her dismay didn't show in her expression.

Just then Jim came bounding down the stairs. "Sammy boy, are you having supper with us?"

"Not this time," Sam said. "Kirsten and I are going out."

"Suit yourself," Jim said with an exaggerated shrug, "but I gotta tell you, Coralie's fixin' macaroni and cheese and it smells mighty good."

Sam grinned. "I'd noticed. I'll take a rain check if it's offered."

Jim sobered. "Hell, man, you're welcome any time. Hey, I was sorry to hear about Belinda. Is she going to be okay? I talked to her parents at noon. How are they taking it? Is there anything I can do?"

Sam shook his head. "No, I think everything's going to be all right. You might keep in close touch with them for a while. Belinda's depressed, and Zack and Maybelle were badly frightened. I think they need friends right now more than help."

"Will do," Jim said. "Has Belinda's husband been contacted?"

"I don't know," Sam said. "That's up to them."

He turned then and looked at Kirsten. "Are you ready to go, honey? I made reservations for seven."

Kirsten, who had been blatantly listening in on the conversation between the two men, was startled when Sam turned his attention to her.

"Oh...yes. I'm ready any time. Just let me get my purse."

The atmosphere in the car on the way to Grangeville had been strained. Sam still hadn't touched her except to take her arm when he helped her in and out of the car, and their conversation had been stilted, skirting all around the subject of Belinda without ever touching on it.

The whole scene served to dampen any hopes Kirsten might have had for any kind of relationship with him.

The restaurant was nice, but the ambience wasn't as romantic as at The Water's Edge. It was less sophisticated, with tables in the center of the room and high-sided booths against the walls. Sam asked for a booth whose tall sides afforded a fair amount of privacy. It was also dimmer, with short, thick candles in votive holders providing shadowy illumination.

The menu was extensive, but Kirsten's stomach was too tied up in knots for her to be hungry. She ordered the grilled halibut and hoped she could manage to eat half of it. Sam ordered a small steak and asked for a bottle of chardonnay to be brought to the table before the dinners were served.

The waiter was back almost immediately with the wine and two glasses. He popped the cork, poured and then left. Kirsten was quite sure that if she drank her half of the bottle, Sam would have to carry her home. That might not be such a bad idea after all, she reflected. If he undressed her and put her to bed, maybe it would revive the lust he'd once felt for her....

She shook her head to dislodge such musing. Who was she trying to kid? It was plain enough even for her to see that any deep feelings that existed between Sam and her were strictly one-sided, on her part. He was doing her a favor by not acting on that lust. The least she could do was play along, instead of making it more difficult for him.

She took a sip of her wine and waded in. "Sam, I know you don't want to talk about it, but I...I think I have a right to know what's going on between you and Belinda."

She felt the warm flush of embarrassment, or was it dread, that she knew colored her face. "That is... I am a nurse. I have a professional as well as a personal interest."

Her voice trailed off as she ran out of steam. Or was it courage she lacked?

"Yes, you do have a right to know," he said, and took a large swallow of his wine. "That's why I wanted to talk to you tonight. Belinda overdosed on sleeping pills, and I don't know whether it was accidental or deliberate. She

wears it was accidental and I want to believe her...." His
voice trailed off, too.

"But?" Kirsten prodded.

He shook his head. "No buts. I've listed it as an accidental OD on her chart and records."

He was being evasive and they both knew it. "Then
what's the problem?" she said impatiently. "Why are you
being so...so *cool* toward me? I had nothing to do with
it."

He looked startled. "Not *cool*, Kirsten. My feelings
about you are never cool. In fact they've been getting too
hot, and that was never my intention. I meant everything I
said when we first started dating. I have no intention of
getting married or of having a serious long-term relationship with a woman."

He took another gulp of his wine. "Belinda's return
hasn't changed that. In fact it's strengthened my resolve."

"I understand that," Kirsten said.

He looked away from her. "No, I don't think you do,
and I'm not going to hurt you the way I've hurt her."

Now it was Kirsten's turn to be shocked. "Hurt her!
What are you talking about? She's the one who hurt *you!*"

"Originally, yes," he agreed, "but when she came back
here after her marriage failed expecting to take up with me
where we left off, I rejected her—"

"Oh, come on now," Kirsten said spiritedly, "are you
implying that you're responsible—"

He looked up and directly into her eyes. "No! Not at
all! Belinda has to take responsibility for her own actions.
I suspect she took more pills than she realized the first time,
then woke again groggy and half-asleep and took another
large dose without even remembering she'd taken some
earlier."

Kirsten had picked up her wineglass and sipped the con-
tents slowly as she watched Sam's expression change from
reluctance to regret to insistence. She hated to see him so

tormented, but there was nothing she could do except le him talk. "So what is the point you're working up to?"

Before he could answer the waiter came with their soup It wasn't until after he left that Sam answered her question

"What I'm telling you is that I don't intend to see yo again after tonight."

She felt as though her stomach was weighted with lead and she noticed that her hand shook as she put down he glass. "Then you do have feelings for Belinda." It wa spoken in a monotone.

"No, I have feelings for *you*," he corrected her. "Feel ings I don't want to have. Feelings I don't intend to let g any further. My associate, Dr. Michael Taylor, arrive home from his vacation this afternoon and will be back i the office tomorrow, so I'm taking a week's vacation star ing Tuesday. I won't be back until after you're gone, s we'll be saying goodbye after dinner."

Chapter Twelve

Kirsten awoke the following morning with an ache in her heart and a throbbing in her head. After Sam's pronouncement the previous night, they'd polished off the bottle of wine while they shoved their food around on their plates instead of eating it.

That had been a mistake in her case because she was a light drinker, and all that wine on an empty stomach, plus the massive effort it took for her to calmly agree that it was indeed best that they not see each other again instead of throwing herself at him and begging him to take her on any terms he wanted, had left her dizzy and nauseated. She'd managed to hide it, as well as the pain of their parting, from Sam, but when she got home she was violently ill and had barely managed to crawl into bed before she was "out." Whether she was asleep or unconscious she didn't know, but this morning she had a giant hangover and that irritating cough was bedeviling her again.

She lay still for a while hoping it would go away, but when it became evident that it wasn't going to, she gingerly got out of bed and crawled into the shower. The pulsating

hot water helped, as did the aspirin she found in the med
icine cabinet. She took her treatment with the bronchia
dilator, and by the time she was dressed and had manage
to choke down a glass of orange juice and some dry toas
the hangover was bearable and the cough was under con
trol. But she had no such hopes for the heartache. She sus
pected it would torment her always.

Unfortunately, after the block-long walk to the big house
she was panting as well as coughing. Damn! She hoped he
asthma wasn't going to be a problem. She intended to leave
for California just as soon as Butch Jackson could get he
car fixed, and she didn't intend to let a little cough an
wheeze delay her.

Coralie noticed Kirsten's respiratory distress immedi
ately, and issued an ultimatum. "Either you call Sam or
will. He's in the office this morning, so call and make a
appointment while I get the car—"

"No, Coralie," Kirsten exclaimed as Coralie headed fo
the door. "I'm all right. I took a treatment. It just needs
little time to work. Besides, the other doctor, Sam's asso
ciate, is back from vacation, so Sam's probably not seein
patients today."

"He'll see you," Coralie assured her.

Another coughing spell seized Kirsten, but still she re
fused to contact Sam. "I'm sure he would see me," sh
said as soon as she could draw a deep breath. "He's a goo
doctor and would never turn away a patient, but I'm no
his patient and he told me last night that he's not going t
see or contact me again. In fact, he's leaving town—"

"What!" Coralie looked thoroughly shocked. "What d
you mean he's not going to see you again? Where's h
going?"

Kirsten coaxed Coralie to the sofa where they both s
down, then she told her friend about her date with Sam th
night before. Reliving it was like tearing open a raw woun
and she had to keep swallowing sobs as she talked.

She hated being so vulnerable and was humiliated by the way she'd chased him, even after he told her he didn't want her.

"There's no way I'm going to call Sam, even as a patient. I'm leaving for California as soon as Butch gets my car fixed, and I promise to see my own doctor when I get back to Eureka."

Coralie looked dazed. "I don't understand," she mumbled. "How can an intelligent man like Sam be so blind? You know he loves you."

"I know no such thing," Kirsten retorted. "And neither do you. I've deluded myself into believing he did, but it's not him that's blind, it's me. I made the mistake of confusing sexual desire with love, even though he warned me that they were two very different emotions. I'm glad he's going out of town. I couldn't bear to face him again, knowing what a fool I've made of myself!"

Coralie twisted her hands in her lap. "Oh, Kirsten, I never should have tried to bring you two together. That's always a dangerous thing to do, but you seemed so right for each other."

After her emotional conversation with Coralie, Kirsten spent the rest of the day doing her laundry and getting her things gathered up and ready to pack. Surely the computer she needed for her car would be in today and she could leave Tuesday.

As she worked she realized that her cough and wheezing weren't getting any better, and it was progressively harder to draw a deep breath, even after her second treatment with the dilator at noon. She didn't go over to the big house to have supper with the family because she knew Coralie would notice her worsening condition. Instead, she called to say she was busy and would grab a bite to eat at the cottage. Everyone knew that Jim's dad kept it well stocked with food.

She went to bed early after taking her last treatment for

the day, and it did seem to make breathing a little easier. Easy enough that she had no trouble falling asleep.

It was dark inside and moonless and quiet outside when Kirsten awoke, fighting the covers and gasping for breath. She was having another severe attack of asthma. The type that couldn't be ignored.

She sat up after freeing herself from the covers, but it didn't make breathing any easier. She turned on the lamp and looked at her watch. It was just a few minutes before midnight. She fumbled on the bedside table for her dilator and medication, but this attack needed more drastic treatment.

Finally she had no recourse but to call Coralie and ask her to take her to the hospital!

Sam had been exhausted when he went to bed, but that hadn't guaranteed sleep. Instead he'd been restless and miserable as he tossed and turned trying to block out of his mind the picture of Kirsten, her wide brown eyes filled with pain as she agreed with him that it was best that they not see each other again.

Better for whom? For her? That was what he'd told himself, but if it were true then why had she looked so...so hurt and rejected? God knows he wasn't rejecting her. He was just trying to save his own sanity.

Better for him? Then why did he feel as if a part of him had been torn away, leaving him with a desperate need to go after her, hold her, cherish her and keep her with him, no matter what the cost?

He was no good at relationships with women. He'd neglected Belinda in favor of his medical training, and she'd sought solace with another man. Then he'd selfishly given in to his passion for Kirsten, even though he knew it could only be temporary, and now he was being as callous with her as Belinda had been with him all those years ago. He'd turned away from Kirsten and was seeking comfort in his wounded pride and his work.

But his grand scheme had backfired. Every time he closed his eyes he could smell her unique scent and almost feel the touch of her strong, capable hands stroking—

The loud ring of the telephone made him jump and he silently cursed as he turned over and reached for it. Damn! Why was he being called in the middle of the night? Mike was supposed to be on call now that he was back.

"Dr. Lawford," he muttered.

"Doctor, this is Wilma at the hospital. Sorry to call you, but Dr. Taylor didn't answer his page. A patient was just brought in with severe respiratory distress. She's asthmatic and needs immediate treatment."

"Put a venturi mask on her," he said. "I'll be right there. Who is it? Someone we've treated before?"

"No sir. Her name is Kirsten Reinhold. She was brought in by Jim and Coralie Buckley—"

Sam cut off the rest of her answer as he slammed down the phone and leaped out of bed.

Kirsten! Sweet Jesus, no! Not Kirsten!

He broke all records getting dressed, and his car screeched into the hospital parking lot less than fifteen minutes later.

In the emergency room Kirsten was painfully uncomfortable. The gurney she was lying on was elevated to a sitting position to make breathing easier, but she felt lightheaded. She had an IV in her arm and a full venturi mask, which covered both her nose and her mouth, to supply oxygen. Little electrode pads were stuck to her upper torso and were hooked up to various machines that measured her vital signs.

She wasn't about to complain, though. The medicated mist that was coming to her through the mask from the breathing machine had made it possible to breathe normally again, even though it was too warm and confining and made sweat run down her face under the mask.

She would be forever grateful to Coralie and Jim. They'd raced her to the hospital in record time, and were now outside in the hall waiting for Dr. Taylor to arrive. Thank God he was on call and not Sam. If they released her to go back to the farm tonight, maybe Sam wouldn't have to know that she'd been here.

The sounds of a commotion in the hallway distracted her. Faintly she could hear excited voices, but they were too garbled for her to understand what was being said. She was telling herself it was probably Coralie and Jim greeting Dr. Taylor when a figure rushed through the door.

Sam!

He was wearing jeans and a T-shirt with leather bedroom slippers on his feet. He glanced at her and strode across the room to stand beside the gurney. His face was white and his hair was rumpled, as though he'd just gotten out of bed and hadn't combed it yet.

She gasped, and her traitorous heart sped up with joy even as her better sense told her this was a grave mistake. She didn't want him to know she was having another attack! Where was the other doctor?

She pulled off the mask so she could talk. "Sam, what are you—"

He cut her off sharply as he accepted a clean lab coat and a stethoscope from the nurse and put them on. "Coralie says you've been having light asthma attacks for several days. Why in hell didn't you tell me?"

He put the stethoscope in his ears and listened to her chest, his hands touching her breasts as impersonally as if he'd never caressed them with so much passion.

"You...you weren't around when it first happened," she stammered, "and I...I didn't want to bother you."

He muttered an oath. "Lean forward," he ordered, and when she did he listened to her back, then put his hands on her shoulders and gently pushed her back against the pillows.

"What do you mean, you didn't want to bother me?" he asked crisply. "Treating patients is what I do, and you've had plenty of opportunities in the past few days to come to me for a checkup. How long has this been going on? I want to know everything, from when you noticed the first symptom to what happened tonight. And I don't want any hedging, hear?"

She nodded. He sounded mad, but he looked almost...scared. As if she were more than just a patient to him—

Now cut that out! she scolded herself. She wasn't going to get mired in that fantasy again. He'd made it plain the night before that he wanted nothing more to do with her. He was mad at her, and she had only herself to blame. It had been childish of her to neglect her health just because she didn't want him to know she was having a problem.

She took as deep a breath as she could manage and started her recitation with the previous Tuesday and Wednesday, when she'd attributed the fatigue she'd felt to the high altitude. Then on to Thursday when she'd had the first unmistakable symptoms of asthma, and continued to the frightening episode she'd just experienced.

When she finished he ran his fingers through his already mussed hair. "You mean you were actually going to start on the trip back to California when you knew your respiratory system could shut down at any time?"

Put like that it did sound stupid. "I...I thought I could hold that off with the medication and dilator until I got back to Eureka."

He sighed, then surprised her by picking up her free hand and rubbing it against his bristly cheek. "You're a registered nurse, sweetheart. You know better than that."

He caught her totally off guard, and her head started to swim as she blinked away the tears that threatened to spill over. He'd called her sweetheart. Did he really mean it, or was it just an empty gesture to soften his criticism?

"I guess I just wasn't thinking straight," she murmured. "You do that to me sometimes, you know."

He smiled tenderly. "It won't ever happen again, I promise." He slid the mask back over her face. "We'll talk more about that later, but for now as soon as we can take you off the machine we're going to register you into a room and put you to bed. Meanwhile, try to sleep."

That wasn't difficult. She was emotionally and physically exhausted, and even though she was sitting up she had no trouble dozing off.

During the next few hours she was wakened regularly for more treatments. It was a relief when they finally removed the mask and the electrode pads and rolled her on the gurney to a private room, where they settled her in a bed.

After the discomfort of the gurney it was like sinking into a cloud, and the last thing she remembered was Sam leaning over her, murmuring, "Sleep tight, my love," and kissing her softly on the lips.

But of course that part was a dream. Sam didn't want her.

When Kirsten woke it was daylight, and she heard the familiar hustle and bustle of morning in a hospital: phones ringing, the clatter of dishes being stacked and unstacked and the incessant chatter of nurses, aides and anxious patients.

She noted that the back of her bed had been lowered and she was breathing normally again without help. Thank heaven for that, even though it meant she'd been put back on the steroid medication. It was strong stuff, but it was safe and did the trick.

Her thoughts were interrupted when a nurse pushed open the door and came in carrying a breakfast tray. "Good, you're awake," she said in little more than a whisper. "I've brought your breakfast."

She put the tray on the over-the-bed table and went back to the bottom of the bed to crank it up to a sitting position. "Coralie Buckley called earlier wanting to know how you were."

"Did you tell her to come and get me?" Kirsten asked.

"Shh!" The nurse put her finger to her lips and shook her head. "You don't want to wake Dr. Lawford."

Kirsten's eyebrows rose. "Dr. Law—"

She turned her head and for the first time saw Sam sprawled in a large wooden chair, sound asleep. He looked younger, less intimidating and much more vulnerable with his defenses down in that uncomfortable-looking position, and her heart went out to him.

"How long has he been here?" she asked in amazement.

"Ever since they brought you in here, according to the night nurse," the woman answered briskly. "She said she tried to get him to leave, but he wouldn't do it. Instead he sat there listening to you breathe until he went to sleep."

She pulled the table with the tray on it over the bed. "Never saw him do that before. How come you get such special treatment? You a relative or something?"

Kirsten could hardly believe it. He'd sat by her side in that uncomfortable chair all night! But why? He'd known the emergency was past when he took her off the machine and brought her to this room. By then her condition was stable.

When the nurse finally left, Kirsten pushed aside the tray table and swung her legs over the side of the bed. She was immediately assaulted by a wave of dizziness, and she clutched the bed to keep from falling. While waiting for the vertigo to recede, she noticed she was wearing only a thigh-length flowered cotton hospital gown that opened all the way down the back and a pair of panties. Maybe there was a robe in the closet.

She staggered slightly as she walked, but she finally found one hanging on the back of the door in the bathroom and put it on. It was a white thinly worn terry-cloth wrap-around that fit her like a tent, but at least it gave her some decent covering.

Silently she made her way barefoot across the tiled floor, and stopped by the side of the chair. Sam must have been exhausted. Even in sleep he had lines of tiredness at the corners of his mouth and eyes. He also needed a shave, and his clothes were both old and rumpled. Still, he'd spent the night here with her instead of going home and to bed.

Her guardian angel.

She reached out and gently brushed a lock of curly brown hair off his forehead. His head jerked slightly. Again she reached out, and this time she stroked his bristly cheek. "Sam," she said softly. "Why don't you go home to your own bed where you can be more comfortable?"

This time he reached up and caught her by the wrist then tumbled her down onto his lap. "I will if you'll come with me," he murmured sleepily as he cuddled her close.

She didn't even try to resist him, but put her arms around him and rubbed her face against the side of his neck. "Why? You said we weren't going to see each other again."

He moaned and massaged her back gently. "That was when I was still trying to convince myself that I could live without you. Now I know I can't, and I want to keep you with me always."

She clenched her jaw to hold back the groan that clutched at her throat. If only he'd told her that before her asthma attack instead of after! Then she could have believed him.

She trailed kisses along his jaw. "And what brought about that revelation?"

He shivered and held her closer. "The realization that neither of us is immortal. That our time in this life is lim

ted, and I could lose you to something a hell of a lot more
ermanent that my own stubborn idiocy.''

She knew he probably believed what he was saying, but
he was also sure he was sugarcoating the facts to make
hem more palatable for both of them.

"In other words, you feel guilty because you think my
atest attack of asthma was induced by the stress of your
ejection of me," she said sadly.

She felt his whole body tense as he sat up straighter and
eld her away from him so he could look at her. "No,
irsten, that's not it at all." His tone was emphatic. "When
got that call from emergency last night telling me you
vere having a severe attack, it finally shocked some sense
nto me. The idea of anything happening to you was more
an I could stand—"

"I'm sure it was," she said. "I saw how upset you were,
o, when you learned that Belinda had overdosed on sleep-
ig pills. You blamed yourself then and—"

"No!" He gathered her in his arms again and hugged
er to him. "You've got it all wrong, love. The two inci-
nts are totally unrelated. It's true I felt that I'd failed
elinda by not recognizing how deeply depressed she was,
ut it was a professional regret, not a personal tragedy.''

He paused and nuzzled her neck before continuing.
When I walked into the ER last night and saw you hooked
to all those machines and trying so hard to breathe it
arly blew my mind.''

She found that hard to believe. "You didn't act like it,"
e remonstrated. "You were so cool and impersonal—"

"Only because I wouldn't have been any good to you if
d given in to the terror that gripped me," he interrupted.
You can't have any conception of how frantic I was. It
ok every ounce of concentration I could muster to keep
y wits about me so I could diagnose and treat you. Be-
ve me, there's a good reason why physicians don't treat
e ones they love!''

The ones they love? Was he telling her she was one o
the select group of people he loved? No, he'd made it plain
that she wasn't and never would be. Then what did h
want? She might as well ask. That was the only way sh
ever got information out of him.

Her wraparound robe had come open exposing one o
her legs and he stroked her bare thigh, unleashing a surge
of heat through her. She nibbled on his earlobe. "Sam,
don't understand what it is you want of me. Are you askin
me to be your mistress?" Her voice trembled.

"No, my darling," he said huskily. "I'm asking you t
be my wife, the mother of my children, my one and onl
love."

She pushed away from him and sat up straight on hi
lap. "But you said—"

"I know what I said," he interrupted, "but I didn't hav
any idea of what love was all about until you came along
I'd thought I was in love with Belinda, but I can see no
that it was just an intimate friendship that was nowhere nea
deep enough to stand the test of time and finally wore itse
out. I thought I could subjugate my feelings, but yo
walked into my life and bowled me over. I can no mor
subdue my love for you than I can control the weather."

She searched his face with her gaze. Sam had a knac
for being extremely persuasive. Especially with her. H
could make her believe anything he wanted her to, but wh
would he want to marry her if he didn't love her? Th
didn't make much sense.

"Are you sure?" she whispered tremulously, wanting
believe him so badly that she was afraid.

He wrapped her in his arms once more and kissed tl
top of her head. "Surer than I've ever been of anything
my life," he whispered back. "Have I ever lied to yo
Kirsten?"

No, he hadn't, and he wasn't lying to her now. She w

going to bet her future happiness on it. "Can we be married here in Copper Canyon?"

His arms tightened around her. "We can be married anywhere you want to be, and the sooner the better."

She felt the smile that turned up the corners of her mouth as she lifted her head to look at him. "Then let's go home and start making plans," she murmured as his mouth captured hers, showing instead of just telling her the depth of his love.

Her last coherent thought was that Coralie would be so pleased. She'd finally found a wife for Dr. Sam!

* * * * *

IN CELEBRATION OF MOTHER'S DAY, JOIN
SILHOUETTE THIS MAY AS WE BRING YOU

a funny thing

HAPPENED ON THE WAY TO THE

DELIVERY ROOM

THESE THREE STORIES, CELEBRATING THE
LIGHTER SIDE OF MOTHERHOOD, ARE
WRITTEN BY YOUR FAVORITE AUTHORS:

KASEY MICHAELS
KATHLEEN EAGLE
EMILIE RICHARDS

When three couples make the trip to the delivery
room, they get more than their own bundles of
joy…they get the promise of love!

Available this May,
wherever Silhouette books are sold.

Silhouette®
TM

Look us up on-line at: http://www.romance.net

Take 4 bestselling love stories FREE

Plus get a FREE surprise gift!

Special Limited-time Offer

Mail to Silhouette Reader Service™

   3010 Walden Avenue
   P.O. Box 1867
   Buffalo, N.Y. 14240-1867

YES! Please send me 4 free Silhouette Romance™ novels and my free surprise gift. Then send me 6 brand-new novels every month, which I will receive months before they appear in bookstores. Bill me at the low price of $2.67 each plus 25¢ delivery and applicable sales tax, if any.* That's the complete price and a savings of over 10% off the cover prices—quite a bargain! I understand that accepting the books and gift places me under no obligation ever to buy any books. I can always return a shipment and cancel at any time. Even if I never buy another book from Silhouette, the 4 free books and the surprise gift are mine to keep forever.

215 BPA A3UT

Name	(PLEASE PRINT)
Address	Apt. No.
City	State	Zip

This offer is limited to one order per household and not valid to present Silhouette Romance™ subscribers. *Terms and prices are subject to change without notice. Sales tax applicable in N.Y.

SROM-696   ©1990 Harlequin Enterprises Limited

As seen on TV!
Free Gift Offer

With a Free Gift proof-of-purchase from any Silhouette® book,
you can receive a beautiful cubic zirconia pendant.

This gorgeous marquise-shaped stone is a genuine cubic
zirconia—accented by an 18" gold tone necklace.

(Approximate retail value $19.95)

Send for yours today...
compliments of ▼ *Silhouette®*

To receive your free gift, a cubic zirconia pendant, send us one original proof-of-
purchase, photocopies not accepted, from the back of any Silhouette Romance™
Silhouette Desire®, Silhouette Special Edition®, Silhouette Intimate Moments®
or Silhouette Yours Truly™ title available in February, March and April at your favorite
retail outlet, together with the Free Gift Certificate, plus a check or money order for
$1.65 U.S./$2.15 CAN. (do not send cash) to cover postage and handling, payable
to Silhouette Free Gift Offer. We will send you the specified gift. Allow 6 to 8 weeks for
delivery. Offer good until April 30, 1997 or while quantities last. Offer valid in the
U.S. and Canada only.

Free Gift Certificate

Name: _____

Address: _____

City: _____ State/Province: _____ Zip/Postal Code: _____

Mail this certificate, one proof-of-purchase and a check or money order for postage
and handling to: SILHOUETTE FREE GIFT OFFER 1997. In the U.S.: 3010 Walden
Avenue, P.O. Box 9077, Buffalo NY 14269-9077. In Canada: P.O. Box 613, Fort Erie,
Ontario L2Z 5X3.

FREE GIFT OFFER
084-KFD

ONE PROOF-OF-PURCHASE

To collect your fabulous FREE GIFT, a cubic zirconia pendant, you must include this
original proof-of-purchase for each gift with the properly completed Free Gift Certificate.

084-KFD

Silhouette Romance proudly invites you
to get to know the members of

The Single
Daddy Club

a new miniseries by award-winning author
Donna Clayton

Derrick: Ex-millitary man who unexpectedly
falls into fatherhood
MISS MAXWELL BECOMES A MOM (March '97)

Jason: Widowed daddy desperately in need of some live-in help
NANNY IN THE NICK OF TIME (April '97)

Reece: Single and satisfied father of one about
to meet his Ms. Right
BEAUTY AND THE BACHELOR DAD (May '97)

Don't miss any of these heartwarming stories as
three single dads say bye-bye to their bachelor days.
Only from

Silhouette ROMANCE™

Look us up on-line at: http://www.romance.net   SDC1

He's able to change a diaper in three seconds flat.
And melt an unsuspecting heart even more quickly.
But changing his mind about marriage might take some doing!
He's more than a man...
He's a FABULOUS FATHER!

***

January:
MAD FOR THE DAD by Terry Essig (#1198)
Daniel Van Scott asked Rachel Gatlin for advice on raising his nephew—
and soon noticed her charms as both a mother...*and* a woman.

February:
DADDY BY DECISION by Lindsay Longford (#1204)
Rancher Jonas Riley proposed marriage to Jessica McDonald! But
would Jonas still want her when he found out a secret about her
little boy?

March:
MYSTERY MAN by Diana Palmer (#1210)
50th Fabulous Father! Tycoon Canton Rourke was a man of mystery,
but could the beautiful Janine Curtis find his answers with a lifetime
of love?

May:
MY BABY, YOUR SON by Anne Peters (#1222)
Beautiful April Bingham was determined to reclaim her long-lost child.
Could she also rekindle the love of the boy's father?

***

Celebrate fatherhood—and love!—every month.
FABULOUS FATHERS...only in Silhouette ROMANCE

Look us up on-line at: http://www.romance.net

FF-J-